THE GENTLEMEN'S CLUB

EMMANUELLE DE MAUPASSANT

Edited by
ADREA KORE

ABOUT THE AUTHOR

Emmanuelle de Maupassant lives with her husband
(maker of tea and fruit cake) and her hairy pudding terrier
(connoisseur of squeaky toys and bacon treats).

If you enjoy this story, you may like to read the sequel - Italian Sonata

For behind the scenes chat, access to 'advance reader copies' prior to
release, and secret giveaways, join Emmanuelle's Facebook 'Boudoir'
group.

www.emmanuelledemaupassant.com

COPYRIGHT

FOREWORD

VICTORIAN LONDON

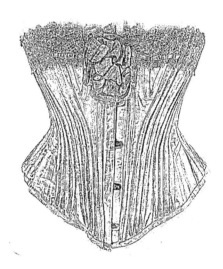

The nineteenth century was a time of prudery and hypocrisy. While it was expected that men would indulge their sexual impulses widely, regardless of marital status, it was unthinkable for a 'genteel' woman to admit even to enjoyment of her marriage bed.

For her to express undue interest in sexual matters was a sign of wantonness and questionable moral character. More ominously, it could inspire diagnosis of hysteria.

In extreme cases, a woman might be referred to an asylum for treatment of this perversion. Engaging in sex outside of marriage made her a 'fallen woman'.

Although sheaths, made from animal gut, had been in use for some time, the use of rubber caps (womb veils) allowed women to gain greater control over pregnancy, and, thereby, over some of their choices.

We live in the wondrous here and now and it's here that our flesh must take its pleasure. Your body is yours and yours alone, but not for long, and never long enough.

Mademoiselle Noire

MAUD

With thinly veiled intentions, Great-aunt Isabella has presented Maud with a series of hand-tinted stereographs, entitled 'Twenty-Five Stages from Courtship to Marriage'. There are nineteen stages before the suitor lowers his lips chastely to his beloved's hand. The innocent maiden, so wooed, turns her face away coyly.

Perusing them in the privacy of her room, Maud smiles. The final image is risqué indeed. The couple, attired neck to toe, retire to bed, the man closing the curtains against prying eyes. The twenty-sixth stage is left to her imagination. In this, her inventiveness is better suited than Isabella can conceive.

She secretes them carefully away in the wooden travelling chest at the end of her bed, opening its heavy lock with the key she keeps always in the pocket of her dress. All her treasures are there: mementoes of her past, keepsakes and souvenirs, and the curios which amuse her, though Isabella would surely not consider them appropriate for one of her years and unwedded state.

From within, she draws out her new novel, hot from France. Its yellow cover denotes its content of 'dubious morality'. She secures such luxuries, wearing her heaviest veil, from a bookshop whose owner cares not about the corruption of young ladies, as long as their coin is good.

Her first book, purchased last winter, was a copy of Mr. Stoker's *Dracula*; what dreams she has enjoyed since reading those pages. Is there anything more delicious than such a book, read by the flicker of lamplight, in the comfort of one's bed?

Maud's imagination takes her to the snow-peaked wilds of the Carpathians, and the jagged Borgo Pass. Creatures of the night, eyes blazing, run through the twilight, their agonized howls stilled only by the sweep of the mysterious Count's arm, bringing them under his bidding.

She pictures herself in place of Jonathan Harker, imprisoned against her will within the broken battlements of Castle Dracula. The three vampire brides descend upon her, closer, closer. She feels the tingling sweetness of their breath, tinged with the bitter smell of blood. Their tongues lick crimson lips in greedy anticipation as they lower their mouths upon her skin, intent on sating their lust.

She is keen to lose herself in the delicious carnality of the narrative, that it might inspire sweet dreams for the coming night. However, thoughts of Lorenzo intrude upon her enjoyment.

To her chagrin, Isabella clearly presents him in the guise of a suitor, as if Maud might be tempted into wedlock with the son Isabella has, with regularity, disparaged for his 'wicked ways'.

His carriage has delivered the latest recipient of the title of Conte di Cavour the previous morning. Though his arrival from Siena pertains to business, he has some time in which to visit Isabella and become acquainted with this distant cousin, for whom his mother has such praise.

Over the ritual of afternoon tea, Maud has endured the torment of being inspected. Dainty sandwiches of cucumber were consumed as his eyes, dark and heavy-lidded, gazed upon her as a wolf might survey its prey. His hungry appraisal, of her waist, her hips, her bust, is familiar. He looks at her through a veneer of civility; she sees this trait in most of his species.

Meanwhile, Isabella enumerated her talents as one might list the saleable qualities of a prize heifer.

He is not unhandsome, his stature upright though his hair is silver-threaded. It is his presumption of her compliance that riles her.

Later, Isabella bid her show him to his room. As he followed Maud upstairs, she paused, and felt his hand slip beneath her hem. Circling her ankle, he held her firm, fingers squeezing a bruise against the jut of bone.

She feels that grasp upon her ankle, as if it were a circlet of iron. To be married would be to be pinned, like a museum butterfly, or to placed under the wolf's paw. He would remain free to prowl. She stepped back to free herself, clipped his face with her heel, leaving him with a split lip and the taste of blood.

Tomorrow, he will find syrup of figs in his morning coffee, and a menu unvaried in its repulsiveness: sautéed tripe with lentils, braised liver and cabbage soup.

Isabella's cat, Satan, is a superb catcher of vermin. Maud will collect his daily victims from the bucket beside the kitchen door; downstairs staff have a weekly wager on the headcount.

She'll place them in Lorenzo's chamber: one little mouse snuggled prettily in a sock, as if sleeping; another perched upon his shaving brush, in mock coitus with its prickly mate; several sprinkled liberally in the pockets of his smoking jacket; and a particularly fine specimen upon his pillow, eyes beady and mouth slightly frothing.

THE CLUB

*T*hose in the upper echelons of society alone know what lies beyond certain doors. Where membership is exclusive, the rules may be as strict as required to keep it that way.

To all intents, the club is a modest refuge from the bustle of business: a place where a chap might read the papers in peace, over coffee or brandy. A fair steak, pea soup and apricot tart can be had: adequate for those worshipping at the temple of the stomach.

However, on passing through a certain curtain, pleasure, pain and humiliation may be enjoyed in the company of ladies who return the virile salute of desire with the same enthusiasm in which it is given. They welcome the bounteous gifts bestowed upon them and, in catering to such whims, are well remunerated.

Nevertheless, financial reward is far from their only incentive. Without exception, the ladies of this harem remain at the establishment longer than is necessary to amass a goodly amount of capital (such as is sufficient to open a millinery or haberdashery).

In most cases, personal interest in the pursuit of pleasure keeps them in continued service. They delight in wielding power over men, whether in domination or in sweet surrender, and their thirst thrills to the added knowledge of being watched by many eyes.

A FIRM HAND

*A*s London sits damp under autumn drizzle and all respectable gentlefolk are either before their fires or in their beds, Lord McCaulay, handsome in full evening dress, is leaving his fashionable residence on Eaton Square, Belgravia, for the five-minute carriage journey to his club. He has endured a dull few hours in the company of the great and the good, including his uncle, the Duke of Mornemouth. McCaulay enjoys a good income and his responsibilities are few, but humouring his relatives remains a duty he must endure.

The only conversation worth his breath was with a fellow member of the British Ornithological Union, discussing the good work of the ladies of the Society for the Protection of Birds, who are rightly intent on discouraging the wearing of plumage in hats.

Lord McCaulay does not generally encourage women to voice an opinion on any matter. However, his own love of birds, to which he devotes many hours of study, moves him to hold the Society's dedication in high regard. He accedes that their efforts in deterring the destruction of almost a million birds annually, merely to provide plumage for the headdresses of the feather-brained, are more worthwhile than those of the uncouth suffragists.

Duties done for the day, it is now time to indulge his pleasures. Replete with the usual dinner conversation denouncing the moral decline of the working classes, Lord McCaulay is ready to fulfil his own hunger for vice.

The luxurious salon on the second floor of the club, furnished in plush velvets and damasks, the floor spread with Persian rugs, is lit by a chandelier of black glass and by the dim glimmer of lamplight. A dozen men are seated in a semi-circle of armchairs; despite their half-moon masks, he recognizes them all.

Lord McCaulay orders a large whisky and settles himself comfortably. The Master of Ceremonies enters and bows, bidding those gathered welcome and assuring them that tonight will be particularly memorable. They are honoured to present Mademoiselle Noire, who will be gracing the club over coming weeks, orchestrating a variety of entertainments for their amusement.

The lady in question enters, walking the outer circumference of the room, where the shadows cling thickest, so that her visage is not immediately apparent. Her skirts brush the back of chairs and she pauses behind each, as if to stroke the nape of a neck with her gloved hand; yet, she does not. Her scent trails behind: heavy with wood and musk, and bergamot.

An unusual choice for a woman, muses McCaulay.

Her circuit complete, she steps forward, and McCaulay sees that her costume is modest: a black taffeta gown, revealing shoulders and a little décolletage. Her waist is cinched tightly, as is the fashion, and her skirts are abundant. Black evening gloves cover most of her arm, and, in one hand, she carries a riding crop. The swell of her form beneath the silk indicates a full figure.

Her skin is luminous in the lamplight. Auburn hair is pinned high, every lock precisely placed. Her eyes, framed within guipure lace, glitter darkly.

A clap of her hands brings forward a statuesque African, from behind the drapes, clad in a leather hood. His muscular body is naked and oiled, and every hair has been removed from his body, so that the muscles in his chest stand boldly and his generous member is proudly unveiled. Its full length and girth are visible, hanging heavily between his thighs.

Mademoiselle Noire's eyes wander over this godlike creature. McCaulay flinches as she flicks her crop lightly at the ebony giant's phallus, the smallest smile upon her lips. The fringed tail end makes contact with the tender skin, but the giant's face remains immobile. She wields the crop a little harder, catching him full along the length of the shaft. The African stands firm, unmoving, his dark truncheon engorging. The crop strikes twice more, each time raising the beast between his legs. McCaulay is aware of a twitch within his own groin.

Mademoiselle Noire bids the giant turn. His buttocks bring to mind a midnight shadow of Michelangelo's David. She commands him to bend and part his legs, so that his testicles hang, huge and low.

A view at once familiar yet disturbing, thinks McCaulay, his finger to his lips.

She reaches down and grasps them gently in her silk-gloved hand, kneading them like the dough of bread rolls ready for the oven. Having uttered no sound until this moment, he now groans, in undoubtable pleasure. Men about the room shift in their seats.

Her gaze scans the assembled faces, seeking out their eyes, ensuring that she has their full attention before she proceeds.

Lord McCaulay lights a cigar, reclines within his armchair and inhales deeply. He returns her stare, which has settled upon him. He imagines that she is admiring the plane of his jaw and his shoulders' breadth, and the bronzed-gold of his hair. He is used to the admiration of women. Resolutely, her eyes remain on his and she presses the African's treasures harder, until the effort shows in the small sliver of flesh at the top of her arm, above her evening glove.

The recipient's moan grows more audible. She keeps her hand clenched for what seems an eternity, every man in the room now squirming.

At last, she lets those ripe and heavy plums swing free and, keeping McCaulay in her vision, flexes her crop, switching it once through the air before bringing it across the tight flesh of black buttocks. Twice more she delivers her whip to its target. Dark muscles contract in response but he offers no cry of pain, not until the next strike catches him partially on the testicles.

Her scrutiny upon McCaulay, Mademoiselle Noire flicks her crop lightly against the man's inner thigh, so that he might open his legs further, leaving his most tender parts vulnerable to her ministrations.

Another sharp crack of exquisite torture conjures a collective intake of breath. The African's knees bend but resume their stance.

Lord McCaulay swallows, his interest piqued, despite his discomfort. Mademoiselle Noire laughs and, at the click of her fingers, the African stands to one side.

A BLOSSOM YET UNFURLED

From between the curtains emerges a slight young girl, blindfolded. Mademoiselle Noire leads her to the centre of the room before speaking, her voice a distillation of seduction.

'Daisy, you're in the salon. About you are gathered several gentlemen.'

The girl turns her head.

'I don't understand, Ma'am.'

'You're here because your behaviour upstairs has been inappropriate to your position as chambermaid. We must reach an understanding if you're to stay in service here.'

Daisy nods.

'You must know to what I'm referring. The offence occurred yesterday evening, at around six o'clock. Tell the gentlemen in this room what happened.'

The chambermaid is trembling. 'I approached a guest in his

bedroom, Ma'am. I asked him if he'd like me to pleasure him, in return for a small payment.'

Mademoiselle continues, her voice low and steady. 'And what did you have in mind, Daisy? Are you a woman of the world?'

A blush suffuses the poor girl's cheek.

'Come now. You must be honest with us.'

Daisy drops her head in shame.

'I thought that I might rub the gentleman, Ma'am. I know that men like to touch, and to have their places touched. I have my own young man. We're set to marry, in the spring. He says it's a long time to wait, so I let him take some liberties.'

Smiling, Mademoiselle places her hand gently on Daisy's arm.

'Thank you for your candour. Our gentlemen may do as they please upstairs, but not with chambermaids.'

Mademoiselle Noire adds curtly, 'Unless through prior notice with the management. There are rules. If you wish to sport with our guests, rather than make their beds, that can be arranged. You might find such new duties preferable, and they would pay a great deal more. It would, no doubt, make a handsome purse to bring to your marriage, and your young man need never know.'

She pauses. 'Is that what you'd like?'

The girl whispers her reply, her head bowed. 'I think I might, Ma'am.'

'That being the case, I think it best that we discover if you are truly suited for such an occupation. Those who come here are discerning. Let's waste no time,' continues Mademoiselle.

She circles the young girl, and casts her gaze, as before, over the gentlemen seated, observing their expression as she speaks.

'You must do as I say. Your hands are free, so you may remove your bloomers.'

The girl looks up in bewilderment. Her lips part, as if to remonstrate. Hesitantly, she reaches under her skirt and petticoat. Fumbling, relying on her fingers' familiarity, she unties the ribbon at the top of her undergarment. The bloomers drop.

'Our gentlemen, like bees gathering at the lip of a succulent lily, are keen to assess the succulence within,' Mademoiselle coaxes.

The girl takes the hem of her skirts and raises them to her knee, then higher, until the top of her thick worsted stockings is visible and a small section of pale thigh above.

Someone coughs. There is an atmosphere of impatience. Mademoiselle Noire is taking her time. McCaulay is not alone in wishing she would speed up proceedings.

'We must see more, Daisy.' Mademoiselle's fingers stroke a curl of hair at the nape of the girl's neck.

'Take off your stockings, and raise your skirts fully, so that they're about your waist.'

'Oh Ma'am,' mumbles Daisy, her lips quivering now, close to tears.

'You may leave, now, or at any time you choose; it is a freedom all ladies of this establishment enjoy. Only those who wish to be here stay,' answers Mademoiselle. 'If this is your calling, you must prove yourself.'

So it is that the girl, flustered but willing, holds the rough fabric high. The cleft between her legs is revealed: two slivers of pink protruding from a bush of dark hair.

Brava, thinks McCaulay. *This little show is becoming more diverting.*

Mademoiselle bids the girl turn, to show her rump. The girl obliges, letting her skirts drop to the front, and raising them instead at the back. Her behind is a fleshy peach. Mademoiselle instructs her to bend further and, as she tilts, the young maid reveals more than she might imagine.

'You're quite delightful,' Mademoiselle Noire assures her. 'Now, stay just as you are. A test lies before you and the end result will be worth any small discomfort. In truth, modesty is an obstacle easily surmounted.'

Mademoiselle gestures forward the African, of whom Daisy, being blindfolded, is unaware. The giant's erection has eased a little over the passing minutes, but what next ensues restores its prowess.

With surprising gentleness, he rests his palms upon the girl's buttocks, so that she might feel their heat. This startles her, but his tender touch quickly reassures. One hand moves to cup her sweet cunny. She is surprisingly still, pushing back against the pressure of its warmth. The dark Adonis moves his finger, finding her, pressing lightly, until the girl's breath comes more rapidly.

Mademoiselle Noire observes closely, asking Daisy if she wishes to drop her skirts and leave. The girl shakes her head. Her virgin cleft welcomes the African's caressing finger. There is no hint of struggle.

Mademoiselle watches with genuine satisfaction. 'The last test,' she announces, 'is one which you may perform for us yourself.'

She motions for the African to remove his hand and Mademoiselle helps the girl, she being without her sight, to a chair. So light-headed is the maid that she can barely stand. Mademoiselle sits her to the edge, her buttocks perched, and lifts the girl's skirts. She eases her legs apart.

McCaulay licks his lips at this stirring sight.

Mademoiselle Noire removes her evening glove, to reveal a delicate wrist and fingers long and elegant.

'Our gentlemen, like good worker bees, are watching, Daisy,' she murmurs to her ear. 'Be their Queen. Let your beauty bloom for them, nourish them.'

She guides Daisy's hand to her sex, her own fingers in parallel with the maid's. Mademoiselle locates the waiting nub and, through the pressure of her own hand, caresses the chambermaid to the final pulsing, gasping moments of feminine fulfilment.

It is a sight to behold: the previously timid and intimidated girl, legs spread wide, pleasuring herself to such an audience. McCaulay is inspired to applaud the maid, and Mademoiselle, the others soon following in signifying their admiration.

Mademoiselle Noire inclines her head in recognition. Her satisfaction is evident.

'Gentlemen, our young chambermaid was a blossom yet unfurled; now, the garden of delights is open to her. Daisy has proven herself highly suitable for the labours commensurate with her new position. She will come to revel in the activities of the bed chamber.'

Lowering the girl's skirts, and raising her to her feet, Mademoiselle's voice is gentle.

'Daisy, you'll go upstairs now, to bathe, and to wait in our finest bedroom, ready for your first lover. The bestowing of maidenhood is rare, so your price will be high: a worthy contribution to your dowry. I'll select your lover myself and will see to it that he makes this night one of sweet and shuddering pleasure. There's no need for fear. You're right that men will like to feel your hand upon them and will touch you in return. They'll do a great many things that may surprise you. Allow your body to respond as it wishes, and all will be well.'

She rubs Daisy's shoulder companionably.

'If, after tonight, you decide that these duties are not to your taste, we'll send you on your way with all that you need to find employment elsewhere. Nevertheless, I believe that you'll enjoy the amours which await.'

The notion holds some appeal to McCaulay, who can see what Mademoiselle's keen eye had penetrated far earlier: that Daisy is a girl of unfulfilled passion, shy and inexperienced, but wonderfully responsive. He sits up a little in his chair, attempting to catch Mademoiselle's gaze once more.

However, she avoids his look of eagerness, searching the room for another: a man whose hair is tinged with silver. She glides her ungloved hand across his cheek, allowing his nose to catch the girl's scent, and tilting his head that she might whisper into his ear. All seriousness, he listens to her instructions, nodding in assent before removing himself to the outer chamber. Daisy's lover has been chosen.

15

DEBASEMENT

For the final performance of the evening, Mademoiselle Noire requests a volunteer. Resolving that he will not be deprived of any pleasure on offer, Lord McCaulay chooses not to dilly-dally, immediately standing to present his services. She laughs at his impatience and motions him forward, requesting that he remove his clothing. This he does without embarrassment, being proud of his strong body. His chest, legs, arms and groin are abundant in hair, and his phallus is of good size; he does not fear it appearing unworthy, despite the proximity of the ebony giant.

Once naked, he stands expectantly. 'And you, Mademoiselle, might you remove some of your garments? he asks.

She appears nothing but amused.

'Tonight, it is I who give the commands, Sir, not you. Some other time, you may have the gratification of reversing our roles. Do you consent to place yourself at my bidding, to undertake any action I see fit?'

He replies with alacrity. 'You may do with me as you wish; my body is at your disposal, and I vouch it will not disappoint.' He gives a mock bow.

Mademoiselle Noire is accustomed to such airs of hauteur; those of his upbringing and education rarely fail to surprise her.

From a trunk placed to one side, she fetches an item unfamiliar to McCaulay: a leg spreader. This she places between his ankles, fixing them apart, so that he stands not uncomfortably, but rather self-consciously, his genitalia swinging free.

She binds his wrists in front of his body with a sash of velvet. His anticipation causes his penis to leap. With a smile of satisfaction, he hopes that the other gentlemen feel some envy at him being the first to perform with Mademoiselle.

However, Lord McCaulay's expectations are soon thwarted.

'Have you ever felt the touch of a man, gentle Sir?' the seductress enquires.

'Of course, during my school days, there were some minor dalliances, prompted by boyish dares or pranks, but not for some twelve years.'

In fact, McCaulay's tastes are various, but his private indulgences are not for present ears.

'I'm sure you speak the truth but perhaps we may be permitted to awaken a memory for you.'

Mademoiselle gives McCaulay the most charming of smiles.

'We are apt to unduly set aside some pleasures, seeking to create an image of which we feel our peers would approve.'

The challenge is unmistakable. Lord McCaulay becomes at once aware of the black mountain of a man and his body stiffens in alarm. It's not the performance he had in mind and he curses her, and himself, for having been tricked so easily. Nevertheless, he feels a surge of arousal at the control she exerts over him; she is a woman to be admired.

Barely concealed laughter ripples through the assembled gentlemen, determining him to steel himself for whatever Mademoiselle has in mind. He won't allow his 'colleagues' or this wily vamp the pleasure of seeing him discomfited.

Mademoiselle Noire asks him once more, 'Sir, you need not prove yourself to any man here. Do you wish to return to your chair and allow another to take your place?'

The lady is all outward civility, but McCaulay feels the impudence of her tone. Whatever she might proclaim, his manhood is in question. He resolves to stand firm.

At this, she bids the African step forward. His mighty hands grasp McCaulay's buttocks, allowing a draught of cool air to move between them. As his anus is exposed, he clenches his cheeks, inspiring a firmer grip from the giant. McCaulay hopes that his face betrays none of his trepidation.

'Our friend will place his phallus between your cheeks, there to pleasure himself in whatever motion most satisfies him. He may knock at your door a little, but he will not enter... yet.'

With his legs apart, McCaulay's nether regions are entirely undefended. The giant locks McCaulay's pelvis in a firm grip and begins the slow rubbing of his shaft along the crease of our Lord's buttocks. The African's heavy testicles bump against McCaulay's own with each motion.

Despite his fear, his heart's rapid beat fuels an erection, as cannot fail to be noted by his seated colleagues.

Damn the woman, he curses.

Reminding himself to breathe slowly and keep his head, he takes solace in the principle by which he aspires to live: the enjoyment of experiences new and unexpected. He can hardly argue that the evening has been a bore. Whatever transpires in the following minutes, he doubts he might describe it later as having been dull.

Mademoiselle Noire touches his cheek and leans in to his ear, so close that her hair brushes his lobe.

'Are you quite sure you are the adventurer you believe yourself to be? Do you wish me to end this?' she whispers, without hint of mockery.

He considers for a moment, before hissing a curse.

'My Lord,' she proclaims, loud enough for all to hear now. 'I detect some apprehension. Let us relax you.'

She pulls over a padded stool, placing it before him, and drops to her knees, settling herself into a comfortable position. To McCaulay's surprise, she takes his cock into the velvet of her mouth. As the African continues his labours behind, she begins her feast.

In light of her antagonistic tone, McCaulay has not expected such an intimacy as this. Her devouring of him belies the taunting of her previous discourse, being most expertly and enthusiastically given. Many a whore has performed a similar service upon his Lordship, but never with such vigour. The soft caress of her tongue and the suction of her mouth are executed as if entirely for her own pleasure. Her skill, combined with the rhythmic grinding between his cheeks, sends McCaulay quickly to the edge of his control.

There can be no doubt that Mademoiselle's enjoyment matches his own. She grasps the back of his thighs, pulling him deeper into her throat.

Meanwhile, the African's movements have inspired viscous emanations, which allow his dark phallus to move more easily, lubricated in its confinement.

McCaulay is discovering that rear stimulation, notwithstanding from a huge black penis rather than the dainty fingers of a girl, is a heady combination in conjunction with a cock-suck fit for royalty.

Mademoiselle Noire's hands move from the back of his thighs to his balls, cupping them tightly as her mouth plunges. His natural inclination is to thrust forward, matching her movements, and, within moments, he feels that his climax may be upon him.

His hands, though bound, weave into Mademoiselle's auburn locks, so carefully arranged atop her elegant head. He yanks her by the hair, so that he might see her eyes and witness the expression in them as he comes deeply, her mouth wrapped around him, lips plump and red.

He sees pure lust: pupils dilated and the glazed immersion of desire – but only for a moment. He holds her fast, her head at an awkward angle, his organ pushed fully to the back of her throat, preventing her from withdrawing, or taking breath. This presumption brings forth her anger, and a spike of malice.

Digging her nails into his testicles, she elicits her release from his grasp, retracting her mouth to the head of his organ and biting down upon it, casting away the power of his imminent eruption and replacing it with pain.

She stands, smoothing her skirt and her hair. 'Why, gentle Sir,' she reprimands, her voice steely, 'you misunderstand your role. Let me remind you.'

McCaulay's cock remains purple, full-veined and potent before him, a little tender from her attack, but still at near full extension. He grinds his teeth in frustration.

At a nod from Mademoiselle Noire, the black Adonis wraps one mighty arm around his captive's abdomen, drawing him close to his own, and reaches around with the other hand, taking the root of the Lord's penis in his grip. Thumb and forefinger form a tight circumnavigation of its girth, while the giant's remaining fingers brush the front of McCaulay's testicles.

To McCaulay's shame, the African begins a slow massage of the base of his shaft. He realises that he will soon be powerless to control his ejaculation, before this room of men. McCaulay's arousal, though unwilling, is obvious. No matter his finer feelings, his body responds fiercely to the grasp of his assailant. His audience is no longer chuckling. Their gaze is fixed upon his member. Some lick their lips and shift in their seats; others adjust themselves discreetly.

With expert co-ordination, the giant resumes his grinding against McCaulay's rear, juices flowing freely, so that he is able to reach some speed. As promised, he hasn't penetrated McCaulay's person, merely gratifying himself in rubbing between the gentleman's cheeks.

Another nod from Mademoiselle Noire commands the African to alter the angle of his thrust, so that his phallus no longer slips innocently between McCaulay's buttocks but begins pressing more insistently, the bulbous helmet probing the outer rim of the Lord's anus, seeking entry.

At this, McCaulay attempts to struggle, but the creature's grip on his member and torso holds him firm. His legs he cannot move, since they remain pinned awkwardly by the spreader. Despite himself, McCaulay is edging dangerously close to the precipice. He feels the wet penis behind him gain some foothold in its quest, pressing solidly at his door.

'Do you wish us to close the performance early, dear Sir?' enquires Mademoiselle, the casualness of her question at odds with the chill in her voice. 'I see that you strive to free yourself, despite being evidently stirred. It may be that you do not know your true carnal nature, but I have no wish to force this upon you if you're unwilling to welcome such desires.'

McCaulay knows that he might cry out in indignation, ending the assault upon his person in an instant. Yet, he does not. He is a man used to his own way in all things. That another might gain the better of him is inconceivable. He won't give this woman the satisfaction of seeing him squirm.

In truth, McCaulay had forgotten the illicit thrill of a man's hands upon his private parts and the charge of a hot organ nudging at his rear: pleasures enjoyed on many cold nights in his college days. That this woman, in no more than an instant, has surmised his hidden inclinations fills him with both horror and begrudging admiration.

Gritting his teeth, he nods his assent.

'I'm sufficiently confident in my masculinity to withstand any task you might set.'

Thus it is that he surrenders himself, allows this forbidden pleasure. At a final nod from Mademoiselle, the Adonis inches within. McCaulay stifles a groan of arousal.

Meanwhile, the giant's masturbation of McCaulay's cock is reaching its final pitch: his great hand working faster now. The lord's member glistens with excitement.

As McCaulay's ejaculate arches through the air, the African steadies his grip on the base of that organ and thrusts his own impressive phallus deeper, shooting his abundance.

McCaulay slumps forward, his knees weak, held up by the man behind him.

Those gathered betray not a smile nor snigger. In the silence of the room, the voice of Mademoiselle Noire rings out. 'It seems that our guest was mistaken in his preferences. His pleasure is evident, lying here upon the rug for all to see.'

McCaulay lifts his head and shifts upright as best as he is able, too ashamed to fully meet her eye but wishing at least to appear master of himself.

She continues. 'If it is a path he chooses to pursue, gentlemen, perhaps you may lend a hand, or whatever else is necessary, to help him in his endeavours. Our noble giant, being prodigious in size and considerate of bearing, has bequeathed merely a fraction of his length to our gentle Sir; perhaps, if there is another occasion, our guest might like to try the full sample.'

At this, the tension in the room is broken, and those assembled guffaw openly, rising to slap one another on the back and make lewd jokes. McCaulay, aware now that he has laid himself bare, shrinks back in mortification, desiring to cover himself and leave.

'Feel free to join our eager harem in the adjoining room, gentlemen,' concludes Mademoiselle Noire. 'Remember, their desire is beyond that of most women. Their pleasure is to honour yours, fulfilling every caprice, without reservation. To deprive them of your complete dedication would be a disservice. Those who wish to take a lady, or two or three, to the upper rooms may do so. For the rest, we trust that you will enjoy your own performances in the adjoining salon, giving encouragement to one another in your exertions, and to your hostesses. Remember the rule of the house, that no woman may be obliged against her will. You all know the 'safe' word.'

She sweeps from the room, disappearing beyond the drapes, and the gentlemen drift off, turning their backs on the stage, thinking now of what is to come.

The African unlocks McCaulay's spreaders and unties the velvet sash. Silently, he too, departs. McCaulay gathers his clothes, wiping the worst excesses from his body with his handkerchief, dressing hastily. He leaves without a word.

ENTOMOLOGY

*M*aud, though a young woman of wit and intelligence, has received a sparse education: several years under governesses of modest abilities, some tutelage with her grandmother, in Italy, and a single year at the Beaulieu Academy for Ladies, where dancing and music, and the art of genteel conversation, comprised the lion's share of instruction.

She is familiar with the basics of mathematics, has a smattering of geographical knowledge, and rather more of history (mostly gleaned from the shelves of her grandmother, who has a penchant for the biographies of great men's mistresses). She plays the pianoforte, and sings, though not well. She can embroider, but has vowed never again to do so of her own free will.

She reads and speaks French moderately but is far more proficient in Italian, having been raised for many years on those heavenly shores. In fact, she has only recently come from her grandmother's residence, where wisteria fragrance seems always to fill the air, blended with the sea-salted scent of the Mediterranean.

Of her parents, she knows little; they cast her upon the goodwill of others when she was no more than seven years old. Having conquered various summits in the name of mountaineering, they swung their last hook over an icy crag and the Hereafter abruptly conquered them.

Maud's academic achievements are just as they should be, since what husband wishes a wife to be better informed than him or, Heaven forbid, to shape such knowledge into opinions; better that she should be ignorant and sweet-natured.

However, despite the best efforts of the world at large, Maud has found herself an interest, for which she has a natural capacity and a memory quite excellent: the study of entomology.

Having begun with a single tattered volume, faded pages depicting Coleoptera, Lepidoptera and Hymenoptera, she is now a regular visitor to the Waterhouse Building, on Cromwell Road in South Kensington.

She first peered into its fascinating cases of beetles and butterflies at the age of six, in the company of her father. She recalls her pity for each occupant, pinned for display. It was no great leap to draw the same conclusion of ladies: similarly bound and trussed, pinned and constrained, with the objective of being admired, in all their gaudy beauty.

The huge elephants and stuffed tigers left the greatest impression on her young imagination. The galleries of corals, minerals, meteorites and fossils were of lesser fascination, though compelling in their way.

Her familiarity with the small creatures of the Natural History Museum is growing, but her studies extend beyond these husks, taking her into Hyde Park and St. James' with equal regularity.

Those who notice her peering intently at leaf mold think she has dropped an earring or a glove. Who among them would guess that Maud is taking note of the social order between ants? Or analysing wasps' exploration of leaf tips in search of their prey? Or inspecting the manner in which a ladybird eats an aphid?

She is still forming her conclusions but, above all, is convinced that their actions are borne of instinct: fixed patterns that take them to their source of food, to their safe havens, to their mates, and, ultimately, to their death, since their predators learn these patterns as surely as if they had read an encyclopedia on the matter.

Her great-aunt's coachman is complicit in keeping secret the truth of many of her excursions. Supposedly, these are often to the Ritz or the Savoy, to take tea with an old friend. In actuality, she does so once weekly, spending most of her afternoons observing diminutive, six-legged life forms.

While Isabella would take a dim view of her great-niece scrabbling under bushes, she is content to permit Maud's attendance at the Museum's lectures. Maud has discovered these to be both stimulating events and indispensable excuses, on evenings when she desires to steal away for her own amusement. Ever under scrutiny, she is adept at contriving such pretexts.

Maud's exposition of meticulous scientific detail has been sufficient to convince Isabella, and deter her from pursuing investigation into her great-niece's 'hobbies'.

On this day, one of many on which Maud has left Isabella dozing before a warm fire, and has slipped out into the world, she finds herself viewing not merely the inhabitants of museum cases but those on two-legs, engaged in surveying them. She muses on what lives they lead when they scurry back to their nests across the city.

The insect rooms gradually grow quiet, leading her through into the gallery of birds. She tends to avoid this place, feeling sad that these creatures, once so free, are now forever fixed. Beautiful they may be, in their colour and variety, but the extinguishing of their life force, more than any other in this building of corpses, imprints and bones, inspires her deepest empathy.

It is here, among the brilliant parakeets and delicate humming-birds, the owls, the ducks, and all feathered inmates, that Maud spies a certain fellow.

His nose is pressed close upon the glass of a case containing an adult ostrich, brought to London from the furthest and most exotic reaches of the Empire. The specimen has been posed in an aspect of surprise, as if the final thought to have passed its mind was one of incredulity; that the obviously inferior biped before it was more deserving of having become its victim than the other way about.

Maud watches as the man descends into a crouch, to better inspect the great bird's peculiar two-toed feet, each with its long claw. She approaches closer and leans over him, reading from the information card: *Alpha males maintain their herd, mating first with the dominant hen and then with others in the group. Wandering males may later be permitted to mate with lesser hens. In defending against rivals and predators, the ostrich may use its formidable legs as weapons, being able to kill a lion with a single kick.*

An urge comes over her to press the toe of her boot into the gentleman's rear, her own modest kick being sure to send him sprawling. Her foot itches to perform its wickedness. Really! What has come over her?

In truth, the fellow is, probably, no better or worse than the rest of his gender and class: proud, egotistical and pompous but easily humbled when shown his limitations.

It is only then that she recognizes him.

Her boot hovers in mid-air before being retracted beneath her skirts. Quietly, she exits the room.

THOUGHTS OF REVENGE

*M*cCaulay has endured a week of near sleeplessness, tormented as he is by the memory of his illicit consummation before a roomful of men, orchestrated by that woman.

His consent was irrelevant, he being no more than a puppet. In fact, he rather wonders if something might have been put into his drink. A return to the club is out of the question. He keeps a low profile from his usual haunts, being unwilling to cross paths with any of those fellows: those who have watched his shame; first, with glee, then sexual interest, then mockery. The thought sickens him.

He broods at home, takes more than his usual number of baths, smokes and drinks excessively, paces and glowers out of the window. His sister, Cecile, with whom he shares his apartments, puts his sulkiness down to an unfulfilled love affair, and leaves him to himself. She has plenty of distractions of her own and no need to be under his feet.

McCaulay's desire for revenge simmers steadily. Neither his perusal of a fascinating article on the birdlife of the Cape Verde islands in *Ibis*, the ornithologists' journal, nor time spent with his extensive collection of pornographic literature has the power to calm him.

Having studied zoology in his Oxford years, he has often reflected upon man's failure to rise much above the condition of his fellow creatures, driven largely by the desire to feed and procreate. It is only in his ponderings of the melodious and colourful avian world, with its beauty and diversity, and its embodiment of freedom, through flight, that he finds the finger of the Divine.

On the subject of pornography, Lord McCaulay believes that term suited alone to material lacking artistic merit. His own collection of books, sketches and cards (some more dog-eared than others) he deems akin to the Venus de Milo, rising above the common fodder of aids to 'relief'.

Nevertheless, he recalls with some fondness his youthful glimpses at the penny illustrated weeklies, discovered by his thirteen year old self, hidden behind greenhouse begonias by the estate's under-gardener. A series of thirty-six poses by a certain lady on a swing and trapeze continue to hold power over him and are brought to mind with more regularity than he would care to admit.

McCaulay's advanced sexual education began, aged seventeen, with his reading of *My Secret Life*, by Henry Spencer Ashbee: memoirs of experience, detailing every activity a man and woman might indulge in involving their genitals. The edition was thoughtfully given to him by his father, to enlighten young Henry before his ascent to the dreaming spires of his chosen college.

He urged his son to remember the wisdom of Albert Sidebottom: 'Love between the sexes is based upon sexual passion and this instinct is neither coarse nor degrading, unless it exists in a coarse or degraded individual.'

That he retains a much-thumbed copy of *Lady BumTickler's Revels*, a joyful romp through the pleasures of flagellation and spanking, he commends to his tendency to nostalgia, the volume having been a twenty-first birthday gift most jovially bestowed by his Oxford chums.

Naturally, his editions are not left in plain sight on his library shelves; they are under lock and key. The idea of Cecile laying eyes upon them fills him with horror. His duty is to ensure that no maggot defiles the pure bud of her innocent youth. Until she is delivered into the arms of a suitable husband, he cannot conceive of her having the slightest knowledge of what occurs in the marriage bed.

In fact, her unwedded state has been plaguing him of late, since she is already a little beyond the usual age. His parents, God rest them, would surely chastise him. He has been negligent in his duties as guardian: far too caught up in his own pleasures, and his personal desire to avoid betrothal.

Their aunt presented Cecile at court three summers ago, and McCaulay spared no expense, in her wardrobe, or in her 'coming-out' ball. There were suitors, but Cecile, in her innocence, seemed not at all to comprehend the ways of love.

In truth, McCaulay had been loathe to encourage a match, wishing not yet to lose his sister to another man.

Selfish of me, he realizes. *I must remedy the situation. Next season, we shall do better. I shall make it my mission to find a man worthy of her: to secure her happiness.*

His own happiness he can barely think on. As the days pass and McCaulay's remembrance of that night loses some of its harder edge, he is left not only with feelings of abasement, but of unmistakable arousal. He recalls the commanding grip of the African upon his penis and the intrusion from behind: at once repugnant yet stimulating. The excitement catches in his throat.

No less rousing is the image of that she-devil, with her harpy mouth around his cock. How he'd like to choke her, or take that crop of hers and thrash her senseless. This leads to thoughts of the figure beneath her costume. He imagines full breasts with dark nipples, the whip leaving livid marks against the tender flesh. It would be no less than she deserves.

To appease the strange desire evoked by these memories and to soothe his injured ego, he seeks out a street prostitute, intending to take her roughly, against a wall, releasing some of his anger and frustration.

To his discomfort, he is unable to raise an adequate erection, despite the darkness of the alley. The trollop laughs in his face, shaking down her skirts and strutting off with a toss of the head, as well as his shilling in her pocket.

FORBIDDEN PLEASURES

The confectioner's shop Maud most often frequents, located close upon St. James' Park, is first-class: quite as good as anyone might find in Paris. Its crème tarts topped with strawberries, thickly coated éclairs and pastel macaroons are, truly, too pretty to crush between the teeth, yet she does so with relish.

Often, she takes her purchases no further than a bench in the park, sitting quite alone and savouring every bite. She first removes her gloves, lifting her veil to allow the morsels to slip into her waiting mouth, finally making sure that she licks each finger of its sugary coating.

This particular day, she has brought a box home with her, to share with Great-aunt Isabella. Her residence in the house is not long-standing, but suits both parties well. The grand dame, younger sister to Maud's long-departed grandfather, while still sprightly, isn't able to go into the world as often as she once did. Her pleasure now is to recall the scandals of the past and to pronounce on those of the present. She takes all the fashionable journals and, of course, *The Times*, which can be relied upon to keep her informed of the death of her former rivals, and lovers.

Her drinking of sweet sherry begins early in the afternoon and continues steadily enough to see her to her bed as soon as a light supper has been eaten, around half past seven. Ever at her side is her beloved Persian, Satan, whose fluffy demeanour belies a vicious streak. His mistress alone is immune to his claws, since the creature is wise enough to know whose hand supplies its daily dish of salmon.

Maud wishes Isabella a good morning (although the hour is close enough upon midday). Her great-aunt has dressed but recently, and her costume is rather deshabillé, but her hair, as ever, is beautifully coiffed and jewels adorn her ears, throat and fingers. Satan, nestled in his mistress' lap, hisses at Maud as she leans to kiss Isabella upon the forehead.

'A marvelous sensation today, my dear,' Isabella declares, pointing to her newspaper. Lord Sebastian Biddulph, whom I remember most distinctly from my younger years, the rogue, has left a significant fortune on his passing. However, the chief benefactor is neither his wife, nor his adult offspring!'

Maud raises an eyebrow. The story is *scandaloso* indeed.

'A modest allowance is endowed on Lady Biddulph, alongside a portrait of her husband upon his prize filly, Matilda, as won the Grand National last season.'

Isabella is positively gleeful.

'Lady Biddulph has never liked to ride, so I hear, and has always resented her husband's pursuit of the pastime. Meanwhile, Sebastian and Archibald are cast entirely upon their own initiative, which I would assume to be in limited supply.'

'Lord Biddulph?' muses Maud. 'I don't think I've been formally introduced, although his name sounds familiar.'

'The recipient is, would you believe, a young woman of dubious background,' continues Isabella. 'In fact, it's rumoured that she works at a high-class brothel! Some place between Belgravia and Mayfair, though the newspaper is irritatingly vague.'

Isabella dashes down the pages in a fit of pique, her desire for details disappointed.

'It wouldn't surprise me if this mysterious, debauched establishment hadn't paid to have this thinly-veiled mention,' she sighs. 'No doubt, there will be a stampede for its doors.'

Maud thinks it best to deflect the conversation, opening the patisserie box and inviting Isabella to make first selection.

'*Buon appetito!*' says Maud, and the two sit in contemplative appreciation of so much raspberry glaze, vanilla custard and light choux pastry. Upon such moments is the bond between them most strongly forged: in the shared enjoyment of the forbidden.

'Have I ever told you of Lady Montgomery, my dear?' asks Isabella, dipping in to lift an éclair. 'Her pleasure in sweet pastries was only surpassed by her passion for taxidermy.' Isabella's tongue flicks to catch a dollop of escaping cream

Maud knows her great-aunt's wild and wicked reminiscences well, and waits patiently, content in the knowledge that the account will be adequately ridiculous or salacious, or both.

'It began with her desire to immortalise her pets, which were great in number, and much beloved. They always shared her bed you know, after her husband died. It's no bad thing in a British winter. Far more effective than blankets, as long as one doesn't mind bad breath and intrusive little bottoms.'

She pauses for a bite of meringue.

'Each time one passed away she'd grieve for months: quite inconsolable. Her solution was to fill her drawing room with her dearly departed and to move them, daily, into new tableaux. Some were fixed with the most alarming grimaces, teeth bared. You'd pop in for a cup of tea and slice of seed cake and find them in unexpected poses: an ancient Pekinese attacking a startled guinea pig, or a bedraggled feline. One day, I took Satan with me and he set about 'deflowering' each and every one of her stuffed treasures, much accelerating their decrepitude.'

Isabella chuckles to herself and strokes Satan fondly.

'Perhaps,' interjects Maud, 'I'll be like Lady Montgomery, kept cosy by fond canine companions. I might try it sooner than your friend. I have no plans to install a husband.'

The old lady splutters on a profiterole.

'Preposterous!' she declares. 'A young girl like you, with such conversation, good health and elegant manners: a loss to humanity if you don't propagate!'

She gives a sniff of disapproval.

'You were certainly not short of suitors during your "coming out" season. If you hadn't returned to your grandmother's villa in Italy, I'm quite sure we'd have secured a proposal for you.'

Maud chooses merely to lower her eyes. She won't contradict Isabella, whose opinions, she believes, reflect her genuine concern for her great-niece's happiness. However, the elderly dowager is from another age. Maud is more than happy to disregard suggestions she deems unsuited to her disposition.

'Not that I'll be content to see you with just any husband, my dear,' adds Isabella. 'You need a man to match you in intelligence, as well as social rank, and with a satisfactory pocketbook. Many a love has languished for want of adequate funds to enjoy life.'

Isabella sets aside her lemon mousse tart and clasps Satan in her arms. The cat struggles momentarily against the embrace but the old lady's grasp is firm. She is about to impart serious advice.

'There is much to be said for a man with a quiet disposition, dear one: a man ready to devote himself to an occupation, and to his wife. Of all my suitors, and I can assure you that there were many, I chose badly. I allowed a flirtation to go to my head and, before I knew it, I was married to Conte Camillo Benito di Cavour: the most notorious playboy of his age, just as his father was before him. Half of Tuscany is probably descended from those loins. God rest his soul.'

Maud, having spent much time in Italy, with her grandmother, has some knowledge of the ways of men. She knows that where the eye roams, the hand has a tendency to follow. Her grandmother has ensured that Maud is not entirely ignorant, for her own safety.

Isabella continues to chatter.

'Your cousin Lorenzo is the same. My darling boy is too handsome and rich for his own good. I hardly dare wish him upon any woman as a husband, although he has reached an age at which the wedded state is the preferable course.'

Isabella fondles the frill at the neck of her gown.

'No doubt, there are offspring aplenty, but a legitimate heir is paramount.'

Maud passes the last cake to Isabella in heartfelt sympathy, inspiring the lady to pinch her cheek in fondness.

Such a sweet, gentle and generous girl! thinks Isabella. *Perhaps, all Lorenzo needs is a wife of more authentic character, yet one also charming enough to bring him to the marital bed each night.*

Isabella tucks a stray curl behind her great-niece's ear.

Maud, meanwhile, has intentions of her own.

'Aunt, I wondered if you'd mind my attending a new series of evening lectures, on the work of the late Mr. Darwin, as it applies to natural selection in the insect world?' she enquires. 'Of course, you might accompany me, if the subject is of interest...'

She knows that Isabella would rather invite the inmates of Newgate Prison to afternoon tea than do any such thing. Maud seeks her blessing, though she has set her heart on attending, regardless of what her great-aunt proposes.

However, Isabella is lost in pleasant reverie.

An elegant wedding, at the family castello, on the coast. Maud in ivory lace, carrying a bouquet of orchids. With her unusual colouring, she'll make a beautiful bride.

'In fact,' says Maud, 'I've been looking into a course of instruction, being offered to women, in the natural sciences.'

A select guest list, of the oldest, and wealthiest, families, muses Isabella, looking no longer at her great-niece, but through her. *I'll commission a portrait of the happy couple, to hang in my salon.*

'I have sufficient funds to pay my own expenses,' adds Maud.

How beautiful my grandchildren will be, sighs Isabella, hearing not a word Maud has spoken. *Lorenzo might yet learn to behave himself.*

'And I may return to Italy,' says Maud. 'I miss the sunshine and the gardens at the Villa Scogliera.'

In truth, she is eager to make a comparative study between her London research subjects and those of the Mediterranean. Does the heat alter their predatory inclinations, their mating rituals, their eternal search for what sustains them?

Isabella, at the mention of Italy, returns to the moment and, to Maud's surprise, declares, 'Splendid, my dear. I approve heartily.'

Perhaps Italy will be a more suitable place for them to meet,' thinks Isabella, with a blaze of triumph, *'And conduct a proper courtship.'*

FIT FOR ROYALTY

*M*cCaulay realizes that any regaining of his peace of mind relies upon revisiting the scene of his degradation. He must achieve a private audience with that Queen of the Night, so that he may humble her as she has him, by whatever means presented.

He enters his carriage in a state of agitation, with a feeling more of compulsion, of inevitability, than of considered action. As he enters the salon, he finds there is no seat to be had. Mademoiselle Noire's performances have gained acclaim and all are eager to witness her invention. He is obliged to stand at the back of the room, near the door, but is in time to see Mademoiselle enter, leading a girl by the hand.

She, whom he has come to think of as Medusa, wears a dress in deepest violet: a shade complimenting her auburn hair. The curve of her breasts is more apparent, her neckline sweeping low from shoulder to shoulder. As before, her face is half-masked.

The sight of her stirs rage within him, but he will bide his time, waiting for the right moment.

Beside her, the girl, eyes covered by a sash, stands meekly, fairest blonde hair piled upon her dainty head, caped in cornflower blue silk. She grips the cloak tightly about her.

'Tonight,' begins Mademoiselle, her voice dripping with promise, 'I am delighted to introduce Hetty, making her first appearance, in honour of a special guest who will soon join us.'

She removes the cape from the girl's shoulders with a flourish, to reveal her pale nakedness. The girl lowers a hand to cover her pubis; the other clasps to her chest.

She is in the bloom of youth, without need of embellishment. Her skin is luminous and her breasts pert, offering an adequate handful, each topped with a rosebud almost indiscernible from the milky flesh. Her figure is slight, though generous at the hip. Her legs, though not long, are sculpted as they should be.

A worthy addition indeed, thinks McCaulay.

'Hetty is aware of the distinction of being chosen this night and, though a little shy, is delighted to know that her first performance is to be with a guest so illustrious; we might even say regal.'

It seems that a member of the royal family will be taking his pleasure.

She guides Hetty to a padded divan and bids her lie back in comfort. The girl's hand continues to cover her sweet cunny, adorned in the palest nimbus of gold.

'Hide not your treasure,' Mademoiselle urges her. 'The candlelight is illuminating you beautifully and it is fitting that the many eyes tonight upon you be allowed to devour your most charming aspect.'

She takes a long ostrich feather and runs its tantalising blade from Hetty's ankle, to the top of her inner thigh, lightly up her torso and across her breasts. The girl shivers and forgets her shyness, dropping her hands to either side.

Mademoiselle lifts a decanter of claret over her and pours the liquid, darkest red. The droplets contrast with her pale skin, pooling between her orbs, and upon her stomach.

Replacing the decanter, Mademoiselle lowers her mouth, her licks claiming each bead before suckling at the maiden's nipple.

McCaulay's groin twitches. He notes the girl's parted lips, her soft moans and the arch of her back.

Mademoiselle moves to the end of the divan and pours claret onto the girl's pubis. The wine clings between the golden hairs and drips; rivulets run between her thighs. Mademoiselle draws up a footstool, to kneel between Hetty's legs.

As she inserts her tongue, Hetty wriggles and lifts her legs, so that she is better placed to accept the ministrations of that kindly mouth, which sips so attentively at her secret place.

It's not long before Hetty is full and open, revealing the slick nub of her pleasure. She sighs, and cups her cunny as the warm tongue completes its duties. Never was a girl more ready for plucking than this ripe fruit.

'I have tasted the eternal fountain, gentlemen.'

Mademoiselle's words are like fingers about the neck of a lover.

The crimson drapes at the end of the room part, to reveal the waiting guest. His costume is nothing if not theatrical: scarlet velvet britches to the knee, with legs and feet bare, as is his chest. A swathe of fabric has been removed from the front of his trousers, so that his genitals are visible.

In some degree of excitement, his organ is almost fully erect, bobbing before him as he walks. Besides an open waistcoat of red velvet, trimmed in ermine, he wears short black leather gloves and a black hood. It covers his head, with openings for his nose, mouth and eyes.

McCaulay peruses the size of the man's phallus, commending its shape and inclination to memory. In the event that he encounters it in one of London's bathhouses, he shall be able to identify the owner.

Approaching the girl, the royal guest claims a pot of honey from beside the claret and drizzles the viscous sweetness upon each rosy areola before lowering his mouth to the task of suckling, like a hungry infant, greedily seeking its mother's breast. As he does so, one leather-gloved hand holds her belly and the other the girl's forehead.

41

He brings Hetty to delightful squirms of pleasure. The royal guest places more honey upon the girl's lips and bestows gentle kisses, until it is all but gone and she has only to lick the remainder for herself. The atmosphere is one of strange intimacy.

McCaulay watches as leather fingers find the girl's cunt and it's not long before she is brought to a familiar state, sighing and lifting herself to his touch. As she approaches her crisis, rubbing against his hand, he removes his fingers and lifts her buttocks high, one hand firmly under each. Her juices glisten upon her sex.

There is a collective sigh of commendation from the gathered audience as his phallus enters, and he commences his pumping in worthy fashion. His prowess meets with the girl's approval, she giving full voice to her fulfillment: a melody echoed by her lover's roar of release.

At this, the company, one man and all, stands to applaud the girl – and her suitor – for their inspiring performance. The hooded guest bends once more to kiss Hetty upon the lips and departs.

PUNISHMENT

*I*n his enthrallment with the arousing scene before him, Lord McCaulay has failed to notice Mademoiselle Noire's departure from the room. It's with some surprise that he now receives an invitation, via the Master of Ceremonies, informing him that the lady seeks his company for a private audience. Consenting readily, and wondering if his chance for retribution is to be presented so easily, McCaulay is led not upstairs but down, towards the cellars.

In a room so dark that it's some moments before his eyes adjust, he becomes aware of Mademoiselle, reposed upon a chaise. Her hair remains pinned, but she's no longer in her evening gown, nor wearing her long, satin gloves. Her robe is of finest gossamer silk, tied by a single ribbon. As he approaches, she stands, lifting a lamp, so that its glow illuminates her features. The flicker of the flame reveals the curves of her upper body, in silhouette beneath the flimsy material.

When she speaks, it's with her usual taunting.

'I'd begun to think you'd never dare return,' she reproaches.

He's within two paces of being able to grasp her about the throat, his eyes glinting with suppressed fury.

'Do you harbour some resentment from our last meeting?' she enquires, the habitual smirk upon her lips. 'In truth, you deserve compensation for your humiliation, do you not?'

He remains silent, allowing the Medusa to speak.

'It's said that all is fair in love and war.'

Reaching behind her, Mademoiselle brings forth her crop and places it in McCaulay's hands. It's a fair length but light. She watches him turn it in his hands, feeling its suppleness.

'I grant you permission to use it against me, but for ten strokes, no more.'

He'd not imagined her placing herself at his mercy so willingly, and his suspicions are raised, but she makes no move to run or evade him. He can smell the musk of her skin and see the pulse at her throat. Her décolletage is barely covered by the flimsy silk, breasts rising with each breath.

He touches the end of the crop to the fabric, brushing her delicate nipple, and pulls the ribbon, so that the silk falls away to each side, revealing the bare flesh: her belly, dark bush and legs. He has thought of little else but exacting his retribution upon this siren but, now, as she stands before him, so vulnerable, he's uncertain. His tongue grows dry in his mouth as he looks upon her.

Hands clenched upon the crop, he battles his compulsion to thrust his mouth at the abundant camber of her breasts, to devour them, to bite until she cries for his mercy. He would graze down her belly and bury his face in her bush, his tongue seeking its plump wetness. His desire to consume her near chokes him.

'I'm waiting,' she prompts, her voice silken. 'You see me before you. I'm unprotected against your wrath. Remember, ten strokes.'

His eyes search her face, seeking there some softness. If her lips were upward cast and parted, he'd fling aside the crop and crush his own upon them. However, her mouth, though full and sensual, betrays its usual subtle sneer. He sees derision and disdain, which steels his heart to raise the cruel whip against her.

The first stroke catches her stomach with a light flick, such as would sting, but not greatly hurt. Her face remains still.

'I believe you can do better,' she states, in that tone which seems ever to mock him.

He raises the crop higher and brings it to bear against her upper thigh, stippling the silk, leaving a tear through the fabric. Her breath catches. Then, she exhales, languorously.

At once, he realizes that he is no more than a pawn in her game and the knowledge brings a flood of ire, making him brandish the crop with more force, sending its tail across the bounty of her breasts, leaving a welt.

She gasps audibly, and throws back her head, an auburn curl escaping to her cheek. Her body unfurls under the pain, resonating with new vibrancy.

The sight of her stirs his blood and his thoughts are again distracted. His tongue might trace the line of the weal, warm saliva removing the bite of the lash, but anger wins out, and he spins her round so that her back is to him. He sends three swift strokes to her buttocks, the whip making light work of her robe. The silk shreds at its touch.

She sighs, and lets the gown fall from her shoulders, so that nothing stands between her and the remaining lashes.

McCaulay hesitates again, observing the stripes rising on her tender skin: faultless, but for the injuries he has inflicted.

Coquettishly, she glances over her shoulder.

He suspects he is merely her instrument.

Flourishing the crop against the underside of her cheeks, where he knows it will be felt most keenly, he follows with another, and two more to the middle of those lush fruits.

He raises the whip again but a voice from the shadows interrupts, commanding, 'No more!'

It is the African, all the while hidden from view.

McCaulay drops back, frozen in terror, reminded immediately of their last encounter. He releases the crop and turns to flee but a firm hand stays his arm. Her face is without rebuke.

'You've nothing to fear,' she assures him. 'Our noble friend won't harm you. He's here for me, not for you.'

She beckons Lord McCaulay to the chaise upon which she first sat. The lamp is beside them, the dancing flame illuminating her skin.

Mademoiselle lowers herself over the taller end of the seat and, extending her arms, bids McCaulay take her bare hands. She stretches taut through her spine.

'My ebony god, having suffered at my hand, deserves also to punish me. Forty lashes, but not from the whip.'

She parts her legs as the giant emerges from the inky shadows, naked, his organ at full fortitude, its tip wet in readiness. She keeps her eyes on those of Lord McCaulay as the African takes his position.

'I deserve punishment for my wicked ways, do I not? I've caused pain, and only pain will suffice in return. Forty lashes, each one deeper and harder than the last. Offer me no respite or pity, no matter how I might plead.'

The African grasps his phallus. To his surprise, McCaulay sees in that face tenderness, as well as lust. The giant hesitates, before entering her, slowly, allowing her flesh to accommodate him.

Her eyes are darker than ever, glittering in an otherworldly fashion. Her mouth is open, forming words she cannot utter.

At last, he has embedded most of his length. Her lover savours the moment before easing back, his shaft releasing her. McCaulay is transfixed by each measured penetration and withdrawal. The African is coated clearly with the glistening of her desire.

Then, with a motion unexpectedly swift, the colossus pulls her pelvis back resolutely against his, so that her cheeks slap hard against his abdomen. Her face contorts in anguish, her eyes close and her wrists flex within McCaulay's grasp.

The African holds her there, against his stomach, relishing his fleshy burial. Slowly, he again withdraws, pausing before plunging into her once more, hauling her hips towards him. She cries out again, but less acutely now, accompanied by a gasp and sigh.

She opens her eyes, staring McCaulay full in the face as she beseeches him, 'Count for me.'

The giant holds her to his torso, grinding against her. This brings forth another cry, soon transformed into a low groan. McCaulay wonders that any woman can endure that dark weapon without injury, but Mademoiselle's pain is also her pleasure.

His voice trembles as he iterates the numbers, the African delivering several full-bodied piston strokes. Each sends a shudder the length of her body, evoking her song of suffering and bliss.

McCaulay stumbles in his counting as the giant's pace quickens, thrusts coming one upon the other.

Her curls are shaken loose and her cries become indistinguishable from sobs.

McCaulay's head grows light, his body present, but his limbs numb. He has reached a count of twenty-five and can no longer speak.

As Mademoiselle Noire submits, McCaulay's own desire grows, imagining that it is he administering those brutal strokes.

The giant lashes harder, lifting her rump to allow the deepest angle of entry. His hands imprison her hips, as he hammers with energy indefatigable. Her hair tumbles in every direction. Her breasts jump and fall with each thrust.

Pulling her fully onto his groin, his jet sears her. McCaulay can barely keep his hold. She writhes, her face transformed, lost in her own world: one in which McCaulay has played but a minor part.

Breathless, the giant steps back. McCaulay lets loose her hands, so that she slumps exhausted over the divan of the chaise, her hair in disarray, face flushed and pupils dilated. She looks him once more fully in the face. She says nothing; no words are needed.

He has fantasized about chastising her but her own enactment far surpasses anything his imagination might conjure. Once more, she has outplayed him, demonstrating to McCaulay that her sexuality is not to be categorized or anticipated. For him to judge would be obscene, since every aspect of her behaviour rouses his own appetite.

He knows, without question, that acquaintance with her will prove his undoing.

TORMENT

*M*cCaulay blunders blindly up the stairs, arriving back upon the street, where the rain-spitted night brings him partially to his senses. Grim horror beats within his chest, knowing that he has crossed a threshold from which there is no return. He cannot escape her image: mouth contorted in gasps of torture and exaltation, body convulsed in euphoria, eyes fevered.

He waves off his carriage, needing to feel the chill air on his cheek and shake off the power of the memories assailing him.

His feet take him where they might, past the homes of men of breeding and fashion: Devonshire House, where the Cavendish family reside behind forbidding brick walls; Stafford House, which is more a palace than St. James' and has hosted some of the most glittering gatherings of the century; Holland House, headquarters to the most brilliant men of the age and celebrated for its library; Bridgewater House, with its fine frontage onto Green Park; and Grosvenor House, with its distinguished colonnades and priceless gallery.

The exercise serves to remind him of the Society to which he should be keeping. Despite this, his thoughts remain with her.

McCaulay spends the darkest hours of night swollen with passion no self-fornication can ease. He finally succumbs to sleep, but wakes soon after, feeling great mental discomfort and a penetrating ache in his loins.

Such is his frustration and wretchedness over the following days that nothing can divert him. The hours stretch, banal and meaning-less. It is intolerable. By night, his dreams leave him exhausted and unfulfilled. By day, his misery plunges him into a chasm of despair.

He seeks understanding of his feelings. Is this pure lust, a desire to possess and conquer, to bring this woman beneath his heel? In part, this is true; he yearns to claim her body and consume it, until nothing remains. He will take her at every orifice, so that his body becomes hers, welded in a fiery explosion of heat and light.

The thought leaves him reeling. Her power over him is a diabolic contagion. Yet, there is something else. He feels her exhibition of her basest animal impulses as a revelation: a miracle of honesty, against which the rest of his life stands in counterfeit. It is as if she has been sent to awaken him to his true self and to lead him on some previously unconsidered path.

He knows that his infatuation is inspired not just by physical need but by something deeper. He hungers for her body, in all its sensual perfection, but also thirsts for the essence of her marrow, to consume the flame of her. He feels compelled to humble himself before her honesty, that he might realize greater honesty of his own. It cannot be love: a condition he holds in contempt. He knows it can only be obsession.

Nevertheless, he cannot escape his conviction that, with her, his life will be glorious: an exploration of uncharted waters. Without her, he will desiccate to dust.

RIDING INTO THE NEW WORLD

*I*sabella likes to take her breakfast in bed, with Satan by her pillow, ready to lick her fingers: a pot of Assam tea, three boiled eggs, two slices of ham, and several of thinly cut bread, generously buttered. It's a hearty meal for one her age. She savours each bite, as she peruses the more provocative pieces in the newspaper.

It is the best time of day to ask a favour of her great-aunt, so Maud has crept in, wearing her night attire, long hair plaited, to perch on the coverlet.

'Such stories today, my dear,' proclaims the old lady, indicating the fifth page of the newspaper. 'The Reverend Huntsworthy, of Smedley Maltings, in the County of Buckinghamshire, has been found to have been warming not only his marital bed, but, in most generous fashion, those of several of his flock.'

She wields her scissors, cutting out the column for her scrapbook, into which she pastes the most salacious snippets. 'He is, apparently, liberal in his love, serving no less than seven households!'

Maud is intent, however, on deflecting Isabella's attention from the fruitful exertions of the Reverend Huntsworthy. She wishes to purchase a bicycle, with which to ride in Hyde Park. It's all the rage in certain circles. She wants a steed upon which to ride into the new world. It will be more than a toy to her; it will be a passport to freedom.

Isabella, though well-versed in the benefits of fresh air and moderate exercise, isn't inclined to give her approval. Times are changing, it's true, but she believes a young lady of breeding should never appear without her chaperone.

She has already been more than indulgent, permitting Maud's attendance at her Museum lectures, and her taking of afternoon tea with an old school friend, in public, although only at the best hotels. Isabella allows this because she knows the eyes of a dozen respectable duchesses will be upon her charge at all times. The carriage takes her there and returns her safely. There is no opportunity for mischief.

'My darling,' Isabella soothes. 'You are of the modern age, I know, but you must remember what is important. How can a lady sit upon such a machine? It's undignified!'

A sliver of ham disappears into Satan's little pussycat mouth.

'I could wear 'rational' dress,' offers Maud, careful to keep the tone of her voice sweet and her face most open in expression.

Isabella knows the meaning of the term: no corset and a skirt reduced in volume and length, to balloon somewhere below the knee; the ankles and calves encased in no more than thick stockings. Indecent! She's read about it in the *Literary Digest*.

Maud has read this, too. Apparently, the weight of a woman's undergarments is reduced to no more than seven pounds. Think of that! There's good reason why Isabella likes to stay late in her bed. It delays the donning of layer after layer and, most abhorrent in Maud's eyes, the restrictive lacing of a foundation bodice: a torture instrument of whalebone and ribbons. How much more comfortable it is to lounge in one's night-shift and dressing gown.

'I don't think so, dear,' answers Isabella. It's her duty to be firm. Maud has no mother to set her on the right path, and her grandmother is hundreds of miles away, reclining in respectable inertia, warmed by the Italian sun.

'Besides which,' she continues, letting golden yolk ooze into a finger of bread, 'all that exertion is dangerous. Such women end up with bicycle face from concentrating on keeping their balance. You wouldn't want to end up with a clenched jaw and bulging eyes, my darling.'

Utter rubbish, thinks Maud, lips pursing. *I'm more likely to end up with frown lines from a life of perpetual frustration.*

The women she's seen on their bicycles appear anything but clenched; they look liberated. Maud is convinced that, were her grandmother sitting before her, she would suggest purchase of a bicycle not only for Maud but for herself too. She does not share Isabella's overbearing sense of propriety.

Isabella glances up from her tray and addresses her great-niece more directly. 'What if you should forget yourself in the excitement and just peddle straight through the park and out the other end?' she warns. 'If you keep your feet on the pedals and don't stop, where might you end up?'

The idea appeals to Maud more than she can say.

DIVINE COUPLINGS

*E*leven days and nights pass. McCaulay is confounded as to what action to take: whether to pack his bags and remove himself from temptation, or to fling himself at the seductress' feet. He knows now why men join monasteries perched on remote mountain outcrops, or the French Foreign Legion, to sweat away their vitality in the harsh desert climate of North Africa. They seek oblivion.

Heart heavy, he finally shaves the stubble from his weary face and allows his feet to take him where they will and where they must: once more, to the crimson salon.

It appears that every member has gathered. Chairs have been brought from the dining room and placed about the circumference, nestled in niches and tucked right up to the tapestries about the walls.

The seating is arranged in a full circle around the space of a central stage. There, a bed has been placed upon a raised dais, scattered with rich fabrics and plush cushions, but open on all sides, so that no view is obscured.

A bell rings to call attention, so that the theatre may begin. McCaulay's heart is beating rapidly, wondering when 'she' may appear.

Two women enter, identical in stature and physique, with well-proportioned hips and buttocks, full of breast and slender of waist. Besides their masks of white lace, they wear simple dresses, Grecian in style, from the lightest, diaphanous muslin. The pair hold hands, fingers clasped in friendship, leading one another. The skin of one is the colour of coffee when milk has been added, and her hair is dark, hanging straight and lustrous. The other is palest alabaster, her hair a luxuriant copper, falling in loose curls about her shoulders.

Both are beautiful but McCaulay's disappointment is palpable. Where is she? It is only when one of the women speaks that McCaulay's consciousness is jolted. There, before him, stands the woman who haunts his days and nights. It is the first time that he has seen her in the salon without the formality of her evening gown and with her hair liberated from the confines of a multitude of pins.

He recognizes now its rich threads of auburn and gold. Moreover, he detects the faint bloom of bruising on her body, though the marks are not obvious in the subtle illumination of the room.

Her voice offers its customary silken seduction. 'Tonight, my gentle sirs, I am Thetis, the sea nymph of ancient Greek mythology, and this is Semele, the Theban princess. Once lovers of mighty Zeus, we stand before you as distilled vials of feminine sensuality. We were born to love: to give and receive pleasure. We shall prepare each other's bodies, to welcome the king of all gods. He shall come to us not as the Zeus of later days, replete with having fathered so many offspring by mortal women, but as his younger self, barely matured, new to feelings of passion. We shall initiate him in the ways of love.'

The two turn to one another and kiss: a caress sweet in its gentleness, lingering and true, as if they are alone and unwatched.

Semele takes a pitcher from beside the bed, while Thetis draws away her hair, allowing her breasts to rise. The Theban pours water across her partner's gown, so that the fabric becomes translucent and clinging, revealing the raspberry areola of her nipples, pushed tight against the muslin, and the dark triangle below her belly. Semele bends her head to Thetis' collarbone, while letting her hand travel down.

McCaulay wets his lips, a flame kindling within him at the sight of Mademoiselle, his eyes drinking her form. His eager anxiety to observe constricts his chest, as if a steel band were placed about it.

As Thetis, she shrugs the wet robe from her shoulders, so that it falls to the floor, and the beauty of her body is fully displayed, droplets of water adorning her curves. Her noble head is raised; her hair shimmers.

Semele raises the pitcher again. Rivulets of water cascade over Thetis' porcelain landscape: across her abundant hills and downwards, to the mysterious valley between her legs. They kiss languorously once more, without sense of time or, seemingly, their audience, Thetis pressing her damp body against that of Semele, still clad.

The Theban princess permits her gown to be pushed from her shoulders, so that she stands before Thetis as a dark mirror: breast to breast, belly to belly.

McCaulay has never witnessed any sight more beautiful.

Thetis anoints Semele with oil of orange blossom, warming it in her hands, so that the sweet scent fills the room. She kneads thighs and belly, and satin spheres, lingering, taking delight in the curves beneath her palm, her hands slipping easily over silken flesh.

Thetis reaches down to the precipice of Semele's secret garden, cupping its warmth; the maiden rocks against the pressure of her touch.

The gentlemen of the room sit silent, eyes drawn irresistibly to the wonderous sight before them.

The sea nymph caresses, reaching every crevice, stroking between her lover's cleft as she steals another kiss. The pair drink deeply of one another, until they fall upon the waiting bed, their legs entwined. Fingers wrap into hair and Semele's kisses travel at last to Thetis' velvet grotto.

McCaulay's lips part, seeing Mademoiselle's legs agape, revealing her plump centre, awaiting exploration. Semele's tongue probes and licks, until the sea nymph is tossed in passion, waves mounting within her. Head cast back, her face shows delicious delight, her pearly teeth biting in concentration.

McCaulay imagines the sweet nectar exploding within her, and her consciousness flying beyond the room, out into the dark skies, transported. A rush of tenderness comes upon him, watching Mademoiselle's mouth open in ecstasy, thinking of how he would love to place his lips upon hers.

As the two lie resplendent, the drapes part to reveal Zeus: a young man whose angelic face is framed with curls of blonde. He is slight but muscular.

The two beauties upon the bed draw him down, that he might lie between them. In turn, they receive his kisses, upon breasts and belly, and give kisses in return. Their hands stroke his limbs, his buttocks and his cock.

Zeus' caresses become more urgent, his hands grasping the shapely Semele, ready to impale her with his divine spear. She meets his long strokes with her own, hips rising to meet him, until she cries out, her legs clinging, as Zeus' seed travels deep, with each throbbing pulse.

Thetis, hungry for her turn with the king of the gods, kisses his member back to life, so that Zeus might mount her with the same ardour.

Clasping her slender waist, he guides her upon his lap, exulting in the delight with which she shares her flesh. Her belly undulates as she encircles him. The divinity suckles like a babe at her breasts, until Thetis' shrine aches for the final lash of the god's thunderbolt.

Zeus bites down upon her nipple, and his juices spring forth, his crescendo inspiring her own song of jubilation.

They fall, entwined, with Semele joining them in their slumber, her legs about those of golden Zeus, her breasts pressed lovingly at his back. Like a painting by Titian come to life, the three curve their bodies one about the other, so that it is hard to tell where one ends and another begins.

So concludes the tableau, and the gathered assembly gives its applause with enthusiasm, some standing to offer their ovation. The play has been presented with utmost delicacy, so that each kiss has appeared to fly on wings from Heaven and each thrust has been delivered with ease, as if truly bestowed by a god.

McCaulay has watched enraptured, gratified to see the serenity with which the object of his affections has conducted herself. Each movement has been lithe, performed with the grace of a ballerina. From the tilt of her head to the pointing of her toes, her body is a thing of beauty, a ship gliding across an ocean of pleasure. How ready she is to lay bare her inner self: showing her soul in its utmost bliss.

As the gentlemen begin to drum their feet upon the floor, shouting for an encore, the three young players rise from their slumber to bow in thanks, honoured to receive such approbation. The approval and admiration of the crowd brings a new flush to the performers' cheeks and they exit the stage with lightness in their step.

THE BATH

The gentlemen drift into the adjoining room: the assembly hall in which they might act out their own scenes, with the ready participation of the waiting harem. The performance inspires a great use of perfumed oil that night: the better for the massaging of tender flesh and the slip-sliding of bodies one against the other.

McCaulay remains in the salon until quite alone, ordering his customary whisky and waiting, in expectation that Thetis might reappear. An hour passes in solitude, so that he has almost given up hope, until the Master of Ceremonies enters, to inform him that Mademoiselle awaits his pleasure. He leads McCaulay through the drapes to a corridor beyond. There are several doors but from behind one can be heard feminine laughter and the splashing of water.

There is a huge bath, above the rim of which three graceful necks are visible, crowned by pinned locks: one dark, one palest blonde and one richly red. To the rear of the room is a large bed.

Mademoiselle Noire turns on hearing his step, her face flushed rosily from the steam. She appears younger than he has seen her thus far, her face stripped of any embellishment at the lip or cheek. Moreover, she is without her mask. She holds his gaze for some moments, her head tilted to one side, chin raised, taking stock of him.

She is the first to speak, catching him off guard by addressing him by name. 'Lord McCaulay, you remember Daisy and Hetty, I think?'

The girls turn their heads, looking at him over their shoulders, as demure as he remembers them, but with something worldly about their eyes. They are also without any mask of concealment.

'Our bath is very warm,' Mademoiselle calls to him. 'It would be a shame for you to miss the opportunity to join us, would it not?'

He desires so very much to be near her. McCaulay removes all items of his evening dress, placing them neatly upon a chair. He takes pains to ensure that his actions are without undue haste, sliding into the comfortable embrace of the water, placing himself at one end, so that the three women face him at the other, all but their shoulders hidden.

'So, you discovered my name,' he says at last, his eyes searching, keen to detect any nuance of feeling. 'You know that anonymity is one of the club's watchwords.'

'I thought it only proper,' she reproaches playfully. 'A lady requires a formal introduction in polite Society and this is not, after all, our first meeting.'

Her tone, as ever, is mocking. Her self-possession is without question, but her finer emotions remain a mystery to him.

'As you can see, I, too, have laid myself bare before you. If you were to pass me on the street, you would know me at once. My own anonymity is now also compromised.'

'It is,' he replies. 'Although the secret of your true name remains to be disclosed, so your advantage over me continues.'

At this, she laughs in genuine merriment. 'Of course it does, Lord McCaulay, and the revelation of my name would perhaps hardly change that, since I appear to control the outcome of all our encounters.'

Her face assumes a more serious expression. 'I invited you here being desirous of better acquaintance,' she admits. 'Since the time of my arrival, you haven't once followed the other gentlemen into the hall of games, to sport gaily with the majestic ladies of this establishment. Had you done so, I would have observed you at play, seeing the cut of your cloth. I know but little of your tastes. Perhaps you have few, being content to follow the whims of others?'

He begins to remonstrate but she moves at once closer, placing a single finger upon his lips. Her proximity serves to quiet him. He feels the smooth skin of her leg brush his below the surface and her hand rests lightly upon his thigh. Water glistens at her throat and at the inviting parting of her cleavage, but her body remains concealed, the suds of the bath preventing him from seeing her form.

He has beheld her nakedness more than once, but those images are as from a dream. At this moment, she is real, close enough that he might feel her breath upon his cheek.

She allows him to search her face, with softness new to his experience. Her features are noble: her nose slender, her forehead high, her bearing imperial. It would never occur to her to consider herself inferior to another being, much less any man. In others, this would irritate him as pure arrogance; in her, it inspires his admiration.

He is swallowed by the predatory, feline green of her eyes. Then, she breaks the enchantment.

'I rather wonder if you attempt to woo me, so intense is your gaze. Of course, that wouldn't do at all, and is assuredly not my desire. I wish merely to conduct a more thorough assessment of you, Lord McCaulay.'

He feels the retort but allows her to reprimand him. For the moment, he is content to be near her. Whatever game she has in mind, he will do his best not to disappoint.

Mademoiselle's young assistants lather their soap and commence their washing, of themselves, and one another. They stroke foam over their shoulders, squeezing water from their sponges. Their heads, one dark and one fair, they hold close, alternately lowering their lashes in modesty, before meeting McCaulay's eye, as if to say: 'Be good enough to look upon us and say what you think of us, my Lord.'

To his knowledge, both are unsophisticated in their knowledge of men, although he doubts not that a week or two in the playrooms of this establishment will have opened their minds considerably. At any rate, the adventure seems to have agreed with them, since their eyes glitter most mirthfully. They have learnt quickly how to trifle and flirt. Nevertheless, they retain some degree of naïve ingenuousness.

They sit now a little higher in the water, so that their breasts are revealed: Hetty's modestly full, with their girlish rosebuds; Daisy's smaller, with dark nipples placed high on the crown.

They cast glances at McCaulay, seeking out his expression, eager to stir him as they soap each other's dainty peaks. Content that her audience is attentive, Daisy lowers her head to the coral of her friend's orb, Hetty twining her arms about her companion's neck and shoulders.

The pair rise to their knees, so that the peaches of their buttocks come into view and the down of their sex: one dark, one golden. Their mouths come together in a light kiss, as if testing how this might be done.

Their antics are rousing, but McCaulay's thoughts remain foremost with Mademoiselle. Her body, naked and alluring, is within arm's reach.

Hetty turns her back, so that Daisy might soap the graceful arch of her spine. The sponge slips and glides, reaching to the under-crease of buttocks and between ample cheeks, water squeezed and replenished, suds dripping. Hetty bends, parting her thighs, so that her friend might probe as she dares. The sight brings a small leap to McCaulay's cock.

Mademoiselle detects the change in his face and draws close; he feels her breast brush his arm.

Her voice is no more than a whisper, her breath catching at the hairs of his neck.

'What is your command?'

He licks his lips and turns to look at Mademoiselle. In leaning towards him, her breasts are almost clear of the water: damp and full, nipples upward curving. How he longs to lower his lips to their perfection. However, he senses that she wishes him to wait, that her interest lies in his interaction with the young women before them.

Daisy squeezes her sponge over the golden down of her friend's labia, then allows it to drop, placing instead two fingers at that ready place, sliding within. Hetty pushes eagerly against the caress.

Eyes wide with feigned innocence, Daisy enquires, 'Shall I, Sir?'

McCaulay nods, watching this pretty scene, but is distracted by Mademoiselle's hand moving between his legs, seeking out his member. She encircles him, squeezing. Her breasts press to his arm, her chin at his shoulder, her lips almost touching his throat. Her fingers reach down further, between his anus and his testicles. The sensation is delicious. He parts his legs that she might cradle him more easily.

Of a sudden, he is aware that her touch may bring upon him an untimely release, but she takes her hand upwards again, massaging his shaft. Her hand moves in synchronisation with that of Daisy, all the while pleasuring her friend. Hetty is gasping, as the flames grow tall.

Mademoiselle scrapes her teeth against the skin of McCaulay's neck, and he can contain himself no more. She wraps her hand firmly about his cock as he pulses, spending his semen into the warm waters of the bath.

When his orgasm has subsided, she shifts to straddle his right thigh, her cunt pushing against him. Her hand remains loosely upon his member.

Her eyes are liquid now, soft and deep. He feels safe, comforted, loved. Her embrace is everything to him.

'Daisy, sit upon the side of the bath and open your legs. It is Hetty's turn to caress you,' Mademoiselle suggests.

Soon, it is all Daisy can do to sit still. She grasps the rim of the tub and lifts her cheeks, urging her friend deeper.

Mademoiselle is pressed against McCaulay's leg, stroking his growing organ with her expert touch, sending his heart soaring, his balls aching again for release.

Lightheaded, he watches as Hetty penetrates devotedly with her tongue, lapping Daisy to the brink. As she tumbles over, giving voice to each wave of wonder, Mademoiselle straddles McCaulay, her sex pounding, insistent.

She slides, warm and tight, rocking against his hardness, drawing him into her. Her soapy breasts crush against his chest and her fingers twine in his hair, pulling back his head. Seeking his open lips, she covers them with her own hungry kisses. Her desire overpowers him, his mouth finding her breast, clasping to her nipple, biting upon the tender areola.

Taking the curve of her buttocks, he feels her shudder and his cock is lifted upon the ripples of her orgasm. She struggles to breathe against the ferocity of the tempest and his rod, fulfilled in its duty, shoots into her.

At last, sighs alone remain, and she holds his head to her chest.

A CLOSE SHAVE

They remain clasped together, neither wishing to relinquish their hold. At last, it is the impatient murmurings of Hetty and Daisy that rouse them.

Mademoiselle is languorous as she rises, droplets shimmering from her body. She steps from the bath, McCaulay's eyes following her all the while, feasting. She beckons, and he follows, allows her to steer him towards the bed, his head growing sleepy now that his body is spent.

He dozes for a few minutes, and when he wakens, it is to find her tying his legs and arms, in the manner of Da Vinci's Vitruvian Man, fastened securely to the corners of the solid wooden bed frame. His penis looms large, already reviving. She places a cushion beneath his buttocks and he closes his eyes, waiting for her mouth to close around his member.

However, the sound of a razor being sharpened against leather jolts him to his senses. There she sits, neatly between his legs.

Seeing the horror upon his face, she cannot help but laugh.

'*Mio Dio, charisma!*' she cries, wiping a tear of merriment from her eye. 'How brave you are! *Quanto coraggiosa, mio piccolo!*'

She lathers soap from a bowl, in readiness to shave him.

The shame of it; how will he enter his regular bathhouse with naked cock and balls? He'll be a laughing stock.

'What an accent you have,' he remarks, gulping as she daubs the brush around the base of his shaft. His own Italian lacks such melody, despite his having spent several months in Florence in his younger years.

She is hesitant in answering.

'My first lover was Italian,' she says at last, taking the bristles downwards, over his testicles.

'He shared his tongue with you,' nods McCaulay, and then blushes at his own pun.

'Indeed!' she replies.

The soap is cold and his erection is fading fast, prompting her to reproach him. 'This will be much easier done if you remain upright, my Lord.'

Grasping his trunk, she delivers slow strokes, the soap offering pleasant lubrication for the job.

'Hold still,' she warns. 'It's not my intention to injure you.'

She proves adept, holding his skin taut, manipulating the razor effectively. Finally, wiping away soap and hair with a sponge, she sits back to admire her handiwork.

'You see, now we can more easily admire you.'

She calls Daisy and Hetty to sit a little closer and explains to McCaulay that, as part of their ongoing instruction in how best to please themselves and, thereby, the gentlemen they may encounter, she would appreciate his assistance. As he is already placed so fortuitously upon the bed, it would be a shame to forsake the opportunity.

He recognizes the small bottle she holds, the fragrance of orange oil, which she pours liberally onto her breasts, squeezing and kneading, pressing and releasing. Touching where he cannot, inflaming him.

She slides her nipples between her fingers, hands moving fluidly. In the gentle lamplight of the room, her skin gleams.

McCaulay admires once more the desire she so readily exhibits, without shame or inhibition. Her hands move to her thighs, and to her private self, fingers pulling open her lips, displaying, taunting.

Her pupils are wide as she lowers her body upon his, thighs, breasts and belly slippery with oil, flesh touching flesh. She presses against his smooth upper groin, grasping his engorgement between her legs, rocking, slithering, pleasuring herself. Her teeth are sharp against his nipples, her cunt hot upon his cock. He can barely endure more of her use of him.

She is close to her peak when she stops, saying, with a smile, 'Allow me to dismount.'

Changing direction, she turns to sit astride his chest, facing his feet. Bending, she shows him her coppered moss, and the cleft of her buttocks. Her heated aroma reaches his nostrils, her salted-musk cave overlaid with orange blossom.

Her oily hands minister to his phallus, caressing its delicate skin, and she calls to Hetty and Daisy. One upon each leg, they kiss McCaulay's inner thighs, up, up, until they take his aching sacks, one each, into their mouths, sucking lightly, then harder, responding to his groans of anguished delight.

Mademoiselle takes his member between her lips, her nipples brushing back and forth upon his belly with each stroke. Even in his most debauched fantasies, he has never imagined three mouths applied to his private parts, each offering its own rhythm of attention.

Mademoiselle lowers herself, so that, at last, he might reach her moist slit with the flick of his tongue. He ventures deeper, bringing forth a purr of appreciation. Her frenzy grows, so that his face is soon full of her.

She sucks down harder upon his shaft, and the sensation across his balls and cock overwhelms him. Hetty and Daisy's dainty lips remain firmly about his testicles as he gives forth.

His erection bursts into Mademoiselle's mouth, and she allows her own spasm to bubble over, sending a spurt of juices, so that each enjoys the taste of the other.

OBSESSION

*T*he girls depart, leaving her alone with McCaulay, to sponge and dry him, to untie him, kissing each wrist and ankle. Then, she dons a silken kimono and leaves.

Reeling, he dresses. It is as if a lifetime has passed since his arrival at the club that evening. He doesn't take his carriage straight home, but rather through the empty streets of Belgravia and Knightsbridge, wishing to gather his thoughts. He passes the homes of those he knows and those he does not; families sleep behind darkened windows, concealed by veils tangible and imperceptible. The world he believes he has understood, and belonged to, now seems false.

As dawn breaks, he turns homeward and finds oblivion in his bed, waking long after noon, to a head hot with fever and a chest of uncomfortable constriction. He is strong of constitution, but is out of sorts. His valet, George, brings a solution of Epsom Salts, a pot of peppermint tea and a tray from the kitchen: sparsely buttered white bread toast and two lightly boiled eggs.

His Lordship will surely feel more himself after eating, and might take a turn in Kensington Gardens; fresh air is known for its restorative powers.

McCaulay is somewhat revived by early evening, although his head continues to plague him, struggling with a confluence of conflicting ideas. Such images assail him from the previous night, bringing a rush of blood not just to his head but to his groin.

His siren remains a mystery, though he has no sense that she truly seeks to entrap him; she takes her pleasure, desiring no promises or declarations of love. He imagines that professions of devotion will repulse her. She will laugh or revile him, denouncing romantic conventions.

She continues to fascinate him, because she continues to elude him, in mind and spirit. Her touch lingers upon his flesh.

He has long held the state of matrimony to be undesirable, since it places irrevocable constraints upon a man. Women, he finds, lack vigour, for all their accomplishments. Meanwhile, most feminine opinions are best left unheard. Even his sister, of whom he is inordinately fond, tries his patience.

Dear Cecile, hearing that he isn't himself, insists that she will remain at home until he is quite well, setting aside an invitation from their aunt in Oxfordshire for a few days' visit. The railway line from Paddington is so convenient that she might easily defer her trip another week.

McCaulay strokes her cheek fondly and removes himself to his library. Her affection is welcome; her continual company is not.

He can think only of his seductress: a woman so in contrast with his sister. Although their ages are probably much the same, their attitude couldn't differ more. Cecile likes to embroider linens, paint portraits, and take afternoon tea with friends and family. She chats endlessly to her little terrier and her exercise comprises a twice-weekly turn through Hyde Park upon her mare, in company with other ladies of equestrian persuasion.

Mademoiselle Noire's exercise, he imagines, is rarely performed out of doors.

The solution, to his mind, is to persuade her to become his mistress.

SCULPTED FLESH

*M*aud, after much cajoling, has persuaded Isabella to accompany her to see the great Sandow. The queue is so long that many are turned away at the door. Fortunately, their coachman, sent ahead, has secured tickets for an upper box. Great-aunt Isabella is in good humour, but she stands in early winter drizzle for no one.

As they rattle through the cobbled streets to the theatre, Isabella's eye is caught by the gaiety of a purple and white striped awning on a new millinery shop. The window is filled with the latest fashions: wide brimmed hats abundant in ribbons, roses and peonies, and slender evening headdresses, topped stylishly with single plumes.

'This is the shop Lady Fortiscue was telling me about,' declares Isabella, craning her neck. 'We must pay a visit, my dear. *The Lady* ran an article on the proprietess last week: a Ms. Tarbuck, I recall.'

Isabella gives a small sniff.

'Such a common name, though the picture of her was becoming.

She is young, and of no notable family, I'm certain. One wonders how on Earth she has financed the venture. However, Ms. Tarbuck's hats are the talk of all fashionable circles.'

Maud's ears have pricked up at the mention of the name.

'These are modern times, aunt,' she comments. 'With a little capital, a woman may make her way. Clearly, she has business acumen and is making the best of her talents. I wish her every success.'

'You're right, of course, my dearest,' answers Isabella. 'We will support her with our purses.'

She muses for a moment.

'Ms.Tarbuck, I'm told, even offers a Devonshire cream tea as one waits. A delightful notion!'

~

THE STALLS ARE FILLED with men and women, equally inclined to admire the mighty Sandow, this modern personification of the Greek and Roman sculptures. The curtains part and the bodybuilder takes the stage. The very sight of him, torso firm and wearing no more than tights and a fig leaf, has several ladies swooning on the spot.

As he performs his routine of classical poses, sighs ripple through the rows. Ladies lean forward, entranced; their noses twitch, eager to inhale this virile specimen. Men of their acquaintance are flabby of belly. Few have defined musculature, unless they undertake a daily regime of sport, or are of the working classes.

Sandow snaps a chain with his bare hands, holding it aloft, biceps bulging. Maud is enjoying the show immensely, but even more so the audience's reaction. They are like the crickets in Hyde Park, swiveling their antenna, rubbing their legs together and clicking their approval.

Isabella is peering through her lorgnettes with more attention than she gave to the opera on her last outing. Several times she begins to exclaim disapproval, then claps her mouth shut. She's not leaving until she sees what comes next.

Finally, Sandow lifts a platform on which a man is playing the piano. He strains so hard that it's a wonder the fig leaf stays in place. Two hundred and fifty pairs of eyes are fixed upon its fate.

In this age of physical and moral degeneration, he is a paragon of health and strength, an antidote to the sedentary lifestyle of the leisured classes. Females left and right squawk with delight: parrots overcome by the sight of a preening male. Gloved hands beat in applause with more fury than can be considered genteel.

Isabella makes a mental note to locate the reviews in the following day's papers and, if there are photographs, to cut these out, for addition to her scrapbook.

DISGUISES

*A*fter some hours spent in deep melancholy, closeted in his library, while reading nothing, McCaulay accompanies Cecile, at her request, to the newly reopened Claridge's Hotel in Mayfair. Desirous of seeing the grandeur of the décor, and of sampling the sweet pastries so praised by her friends, she coaxes him into the carriage. They enter the grand hall at four in the afternoon.

Cecile exclaims on the beautiful marble of the flooring and the sweep of the grand staircase, as they walk through to the dining room in which tea is served. McCaulay eyes the finger sandwiches, éclairs and cream tarts with little appetite, although Cecile is all praise and clearly enjoying their outing. He smiles fondly, happy at least that she is so easily contented.

His sister isn't the only female in London eager to see the hotel in its refurbished state. The central court is brimming with frivolous simpletons and superfluous piffle. Fortunately, the orchestra is excellent, so he is spared the pain of eavesdropping on the conversations about him.

He finds himself seeking out hair colour. Two ladies boast locks approximate in shade to those of Mademoiselle Noire, but neither has the same rich luster, and their skin lacks luminosity. In fact, there isn't a woman here whom he would call beautiful (apart from his darling Cecile). Several are pretty, but simpering; most are decidedly plain, in his opinion. Has he always been so choosy?

He recalls an amour he entertained here a few seasons past: an actress lesser known at the time, but now making her name on the New York stages, he is told. She would order caviar, oysters and champagne.

The affair amused him well enough, until he discovered that he wasn't the only suitor paying handsomely for her company. She is the last woman to have extracted from him the purchase of jewellery. Of course, it hardly matters now. Many a man has lost his head between flattery and a smutty suggestion.

It is the hope of success that leads men to this end, although the wisest of women know that the chase is more profitable, on both sides, if prolonged. Like military generals, women understand that, once a castle's gates are unlocked, there is no need for further siege.

Their tea drunk, and Cecile happy at having exchanged pleasantries with several ladies of note, the siblings return to their carriage. They have hardly reached Grosvenor Square before an upturned face catches McCaulay's attention, in the crowd, upon the pavement.

Banging on the ceiling, so that their coachman might stop, he kisses Cecile upon the brow, offers profuse apologies, and leaps down, adeptly avoiding the collected filth of the gutter.

He looks about him, certain that he has recognized her, but no lady visible meets her description. Then, he sees the familiar figure, with distinctive hair tucked under a cap, just a few locks escaping. She's wearing trousers of rough cloth, heavy boots, waistcoat, jacket, and a scarf closely about her neck, so that her face is barely visible. Disappearing down Audley Street, she weaves between pedestrians, obliging him to quicken his pace.

He's almost upon her when she turns and sees him, surprise and irritation crossing her face. She begins to run, dodging down Mount Street and almost knocking into the flower sellers, who deliver ripe rebuke.

McCaulay keeps her in sight, though with difficulty. She turns left into Park Street, runs a few paces more, and disappears into a narrow opening. He's somewhat familiar with these streets; the Dorchester Hotel is nearby, as is the entrance to Hyde Park, off Park Lane.

Entering the alleyway, carefully avoiding curds of vomit, he's unable to spot her, and wonders if she has already exited at the other end, back onto Audley Street. He takes a few steps more, drawing level with barrels of ale stacked against the wall, and discovers her, crouched among foul-smelling refuse.

Her beauty is all the more dazzling in this low and dirty place, nauseating in its odour, habituated more often by the beer-bloated and sodden-eyed.

She's soon on her feet, making to flee, but he grabs her shoulder, holding her fast. The material of her jacket is so very coarse that he wonders how she can bear it. She turns from him, refusing to meet his eye, clearly unhappy that he has come upon her.

'My dear Mademoiselle,' he begins, curiosity in his voice, and the softness of one who cares. 'Why are you dressed this way? What can be the reason? And why must you run from me?'

She makes no further attempt to bolt. However, her voice is full of annoyance.

'Lord McCaulay, it may surprise you to discover that some like to wander London without being recognized. My costume is surely evidence that I'm not taking the air as a genteel young woman, for which I would require a chaperone. I prefer to walk alone, being of independent mind. Let me be, and I shall continue.'

Her demeanour is so earnest that he cannot help but laugh. Irked that her fancy dress provides him with such amusement, she eyes him with petulance.

'Of course,' he replies, steadying his expression to avoid more offence. 'It's an exceedingly clever idea: one I may adopt myself.'

'There's no need to mock me,' she answers. 'You are a man: to wit, there are no restrictions placed upon you. You're free to come and go as you please; nobody will stop you.'

He sees now that there is more to her irritation than simple annoyance at having been caught.

'How often do you assume this boyish identity?' he asks.

She doesn't answer immediately, considering how much of her secret to share. At last, she admits that this is her second outing, and the first lasted a mere five minutes before she returned to the safety of her residence.

'It's perhaps not the solution I hoped for,' she reflects.

'Nevertheless, the costume suits you well, young garçon.' McCaulay smiles.

'I'm in no mood for jest,' she retorts, moving to withdraw.

He reaches out, detaining her once more, turning her towards him. She looks up in defiance, but his eyes smile in amusement, and with affection, so she raises her mouth, to take a kiss.

'Now I must leave you, Lord McCaulay. I'm sure you have other calls upon your time.'

She begins to walk away but McCaulay spins her about, and wraps her in a firm embrace, meeting her lips with sweetness, and urgency, as if he might never lay eyes upon her again.

Making no effort to remove herself, she moves her hands within his coat, lifting his shirt so that she might find the bare skin of his back.

Her touch thrills him, sending a jolt to his groin, but he hesitates, remembering that they stand in a public place. Though dusk is falling, obscuring them somewhat from view, were someone to call an officer of the police, confinement in a cell might await him. Being found with a 'boy' would require bribery; even then, he might find the story leaked to the newspapers.

As if reading his mind, she throws forth the challenge. 'My Lord, you're brave enough to accost me in a darkened, foul alleyway, but does your courage take you any further?'

She strokes his growing erection through the serge wool of his trousers, finds the buttons and inserts her hand, cool against the heat of him. What manner of woman is she? At every meeting, he begins under the illusion of having the upper hand and, each time, she so swiftly educates him to the contrary.

She gazes directly into his eyes, and he knows that she sees there the look of a man spellbound, obsessed.

Despite the proximity of passers-by, he moves his hands swiftly, unbuttoning her rough-hewn britches and untying the cotton bloomers beneath. Pushing aside the confines of the fabric, he enters her with his fingers. Her breath is already coming quickly, she being eager to receive him.

He guides his phallus between her legs, its head nudging at her, and places his hands beneath her buttocks. Her movement is restricted, but she angles herself to him, eager to facilitate their union. His shaft presses against the most sensitive part of her, each penetration bringing a wave of pleasure. Her encouragement is loud enough for him to fear drawing attention from busy Audley Street.

The danger of the situation adds great frisson as he spears her, incited by her hunger and his determination to demonstrate that he can meet any trial she sets before him. She clenches and he brings his mouth upon hers, attempting to stifle her cries. His crisis follows close, his cock pulsing.

They gather themselves into a decent state, share a knowing smile, and exit from opposing ends of the alley.

ACHILLES HEEL

*M*cCaulay takes a short cut through Hyde Park, past the statue of Achilles, created in likeness to some figure on the Monte Cavallo in Rome. It is a sculpture he has always admired, the hero's body appearing too lifelike to be formed merely from stone. Shield upheld and sword in hand, he stands in defiance, ready for war.

McCaulay, vain and egotistical as he is, has never presumed to compare himself with the majesty of the demigod, dipped in the River Styx to render him invincible, but for the heel by which his mother held him. Now, he feels some affinity with the noble warrior, whose pride and courage led him into the thick of danger at Troy.

His battle is less tangible but he feels it nonetheless: an inner conflict, in which his head and heart conduct their own havoc. As for his Achilles heel, her name remains unknown to him, despite her face being etched upon his consciousness. McCaulay stands, for how long he cannot tell, as pedestrians bustle past. The wind has picked up and drizzle is descending. At last, he turns homeward, the final leaves of autumn eddying about his feet.

He passes through Hyde Park. In fine weather, the broad avenue of 'Rotten Row' attracts ladies and gentlemen of fashion, wealth and celebrity. It leads off into the darkness, his own path stretching similarly before him. He rarely thinks of the future, or the inevitable change brought by age but, now, he imagines growing older, dissatisfied, without hope, passionless and withered.

In the summer months, the bridleway is crowded with equestrians, creating a scene of brilliance, pomp and splendour; tonight, it is dank and gloomy. When winter's frost bites, the Park glitters. Then, skaters take to the frozen Serpentine, illuminated by torchlight.

Many a love affair has been nursed in these acres, fair young men seeking out a certain rosy cheek, to be greeted by blushes and downcast lashes. A lady might drop a glove and bestow a smile. Such assignations oft remain furtive, ultimately foiled by a matchmaking matriarch, caring nothing for the secret wishes of youthful hearts.

He has thought to make Mademoiselle Noire his sometime mistress, but he realizes that it would never be sufficient. He must possess her completely. She will be his torch in the darkness: no other exists for him. His ardour won't be thwarted.

A ginger tom shoots past. McCaulay clutches his coat and makes towards the elaborate iron gates. He hurries past Apsley House: one time residence of the 'hero of a hundred fights' – the Duke of Wellington. The monument to his great deeds stands in front of the drawing room windows. If he had, in modesty, forgotten his own greatness, he might have looked upon it, and been reminded.

McCaulay passes out onto Grosvenor Place and through Belgravia. As he enters Eaton Square, fog is rolling in from the direction of the Thames. The interior of his residence appears less welcoming than usual, although the fires and lamps have been lit. Heading towards his room, to dress for dinner, he stops at his sister's door, knocking gently.

Cecile calls for him to enter, and he finds her at her dressing table, her maid arranging her hair. She would never think to question him, but he feels compelled to explain his hasty removal from the carriage. Sensing that he has something heartfelt to impart, she dismisses Alice and turns to give him her full attention.

'What would you say, sister, were I to tell you that I have fallen in love?'

She is first incredulous, then, seeing the earnest look upon his face, claps her hands in delight.

'Nothing would bring me greater delight, Henry, than to see you happily settled.' She rises to hug him. 'I doubted that the day would ever come. How many beautiful women, of good breeding and charm, have you toyed with? And not one has captured your heart.'

Her words are as he expected, she being so generous of nature.

'That you have taken time to choose wisely is to your credit, dear brother. My heart yearns to meet the object of your admiration, that I might call her sister.'

'What if my bride were not of aristocratic family, Cecile?' he asks.

She gives him the simplest of answers. 'Regardless of her birth, dearest, if she is the other half of your soul she will be a lady indeed. Your good taste and discernment has surely selected a woman of substance, refinement and intelligence. I cannot believe it would be otherwise.'

Her words are a comfort. Certainly, whatever her name or status in society, Mademoiselle Noire lacks neither brains nor imagination. Her conversation is eloquent, her spirit admirable and her bearing noble. Perhaps all may be well.

Cecile, sensing her brother's anxiety, clasps his hand. 'I would receive any you held in esteem with deference and affection, treating her as my closest friend and confidante.'

He returns the squeeze of her fingers; he is blessed indeed to have such a sister.

However, he remains doubtful that his Queen of the Night has any notion of marriage, much less, that she might wish to accept an overture from him.

McCaulay takes leave of Cecile with his customary kiss upon her forehead and promises to join her downstairs in good time.

MISTRESSES

*I*t is Maud's birthday, for which her great-aunt has been
persuaded to accompany her to the Café Royal: a place not
only to dine but to be seen. The central Domino Room, with its
golden goddesses and garlands, its painted cupids and burnished gild-
ing, is filled with fragrant perfumes and laughter. The curtains are
drawn and the candles lit, the flames reflected infinitely in the elaborate mirrors. The air is thick with an atmosphere of Bohemia and
tobacco smoke.

Isabella is shortsighted, which is just as well. The far corner is
occupied by a certain set: poets and artists. Isabella, despite her rela-
tive open-mindedness and delight in all that is scandalous, would call
them sodomites and rogues. Maud refrains from judgment, thinking
them glamorous, and wonderfully amusing.

The hour isn't late but they are so full of absinthe that one of their
company is hallucinating, calling out farewell to his mother as he sets

off to sea. Other diners look on in bemusement, only a few with vexation. One generally expects such things at the Café Royal.

'What's the commotion?' demands Isabella. She's just begun her consommé veau and doesn't like being disturbed while eating.

Maud is always ready with a story.

'I think they're rehearsing for a new play. They're famous actors, from the Shaftsbury Theatre. Something Shakespearean...'

'Hmmm,' says Isabella, peering in their direction. 'A dining room isn't the place for Shakespeare... Ah, the filets de sole Orly!'

The fish is splendid, accompanied by pommes rissoles and petit pois. Since the occasion is celebratory, she and Maud are also enjoying a bottle of Champagne Perrier-Jouët. By the time their mousse glacée has been devoured and a small plate of cheeses is before them, Isabella is in a state of perfect bonhomie, reminiscing upon her youth, and the subject of dinner guests.

'Such wonderful evenings we had, the Conte and I. Our Torta Barozzi was unsurpassed, making it the greatest torture to resist over-indulgence.'

Maud is familiar with the treat. Her grandmother's cook makes this particular cake every Saturday, rich in almonds and bittersweet chocolate.

Isabella continues, 'Of course, the most difficult task lay in deciding where to seat people. Wives and husbands, naturally, were never placed in close proximity, to avoid curbing their fun. Meanwhile, mistresses, of which some had more than their fair share, had to be located neither too far nor too near.'

Her eyes glitter wickedly.

'One evening, on being quite occupied by the state of the struffoli (as you know, my dear Maud, the citrus glaze for the fried dough must be laced with toasted hazelnuts – walnuts simply won't do) I seated the Duca di San Orvieta between two of his mistresses, with the Duchessa opposite. The trollops fought over his attentions, above the table and below, like squid extracting a mollusc from its shell. The poor man hardly ate a bite.'

Isabella's smile is nothing short of devilish.

'The Duchessa's words to me afterwards were exquisitely colourful.'

Maud squeezes Isabella's hand affectionately; besides her grandmother, there is no one she loves more.

During the carriage ride home, her great-aunt's head begins to nod.

Maud leans over to whisper, 'Now, don't forget, I have the next lecture on Mr Darwin's work to attend tomorrow evening.'

'What's that, my dear?' says Isabella, her eyes fluttering open. 'Another lecture? So soon?'

'They are extremely fascinating,' asserts Maud. 'I'm learning more than you can imagine...'

Isabella's chin is once more upon her chest.

'In fact,' muses Maud, 'I'm having a splendid birthday week.'

IN EMULATION OF MESSALINA

*M*cCaulay returns to his club the following evening, determined that he must speak to Mademoiselle Noire, and make his feelings known.

No doubt she'll refuse, he worries. *I'll entreat her to reconsider. It would be madness to think that she'll lack terms of her own. Naturally, I'll examine any proposal, although her continued exhibition of herself I cannot countenance.*

He finds a place upon a side sofa, away from the main throng.

When Mademoiselle enters, she has never looked more regal, wearing a dress of crimson velvet, her porcelain shoulders fully exposed, her cleavage displayed to utmost advantage. Her auburn hair appears set with stars, being pinned with diamantes, each catching the light.

She begins her address. 'Gentlemen, you know well the delight of watching a fair bottom wriggle upon a manly piston – your own or that of another!'

Merry agreement ripples among those gathered.

'What joy it is to witness such coupling, spurring on the efforts of others, offering encouragement as you watch appreciatively, waiting your turn.'

She pauses, allowing the rosy image to permeate.

'Some might say that lusts are best inflamed by watching ladies coax one another, with gentle fondles or harsher play. Others prefer a girl to be coy, since modesty has its appeal and men like to hunt. A woman too willing is perhaps no sport. Who among you has not thrilled to overcome seeming resistance? The ladies of our harem know you well, gentlemen, acting the virgin or the whore, as suits the occasion.'

How clever she is, McCaulay finds himself thinking. *She knows us perhaps better than we know ourselves.*

Her voice, low and seductive, continues. 'Tonight, we bid farewell to Evaline, who has been your sporting companion these last twelve months. You have attended to her pleasure as generously as she has to yours, most liberally, and in every manner.'

Mademoiselle here allows the gentlemen to conjure forth their own recollections of the majestic Evaline.

'She is soon to enter the sacred union of marriage and plans to put aside, with some reluctance, her life of adventure within these walls. To mark her departure, she has requested the honour of your participation in a special performance: no less than the reenactment of Messalina's orgy.'

A murmur of approval travels the room.

'The Roman Emperor Claudius' wife, being insatiable of appetite and immensely competitive, challenged the well-known prostitute Scylla to a contest, to see who might fulfil the lusts of the greatest number of men. Messalina demonstrated herself to be the greater whore, continuing long into the night, obliging the most varied of demands. This evening, Evaline will be without challenge, since we humbly acknowledge her as the foremost lady of this establishment.'

Having received such an introduction, guaranteed to whet the appetite, the lady herself enters, dressed fittingly in a Roman toga, her chestnut hair braided and looped in the style made famous by Messalina of old.

She promenades sedately, appraising her suitors. Satisfied at last that all attention is hers, she reclines comfortably upon the cushioned day bed in the centre of the room. Inch by inch, she raises her skirts, revealing the pale skin of her thighs. She opens her graceful legs, that her forest, lush and curling, might be admired.

Evaline parts the moist entrance to this garden of pleasure. Her fingers are adept and skillful, and it seems that perhaps she has no need of another, her breath ragged from her own touch. It is then that she summons forth her first lover, with a simple crook of her finger.

The gentleman remains fully clothed, taking out only those parts essential to the act, already in a condition ready to conquer. Grasping his organ, he lowers himself upon her, eager to sate his desire.

She tilts her hips, and his rod gains the first toast of the night, pushing slowly, and then with greater acceleration. She closes her eyes, embracing the sensual delight of their coupling, knowing that she will enjoy every man gathered. The night can end in one fashion alone: a feast in which each will enjoy her body.

Within the shortest time, her lover lets forth a groan of satisfaction and Evaline's smile gives proof of her own. She kneels upon the divan, offering her buttocks. Her next suitor pours champagne down the cleft, before bending his head to drink, rubbing his bearded face against the length of her valley, tickling and teasing her with his hairy chin, his nose and mouth. The sucking of liquid from her secret folds makes the lady breathless with desire. She is eager to welcome stricter ministrations.

The gentleman is joined by another, keen to sample her velvet passage. The two share her, stroking with agile tongues, keeping her pleasure simmering, until she is quite beside herself, crying out for fulfilment.

At last, bringing forth their engorged organs, the gentlemen take turns to deliver ever-fiercer strokes, shaking free the lady's breasts from her draping costume.

Her face flushed and radiant, Evaline submits joyfully, reveling in the battle waged at her rump, and letting forth shrieks of encouragement, excited all the more by the knowledge of so many eyes witnessing her arousal, and final culmination of ecstasy. Her cries bring forth those of her gentlemen with due alacrity.

Resting for a moment, Evaline removes her robe, to fully reveal her naked beauty. Reclining, she cups her generous breasts, before allowing her touch to stray to her rounded belly and, once more, to the mount of her Venus.

She teases those gathered, pushing her fingertips inside, so that they emerge glistening with juices. These she sucks, parting her legs wider each time, as she gathers her succulent harvest.

Evaline motions for the gentlemen gathered about her to pleasure themselves. The lady's undulations, most enchanting to behold, summon joyous eruptions from her admirers. These, she rubs provocatively into her thighs, breasts and stomach.

In various states of undress, those about her join in her fondling, lowering their mouths to her nipples, to her arms and legs, holding each limb captive, about the wrist or ankle, each suitor taking care to deliver only the most welcome of sensations.

A cushion is placed under her dainty buttocks, so that her sweet jewel is best able to invite attention. One after another, her lovers take their turn in delighting her, supping at this tastiest of morsels.

Hands and lips continue to rove her body in tender fashion. Her snowy breasts are squeezed and softly pinched while teeth graze her skin. Her nipples ache for those tweaks and bites, just as her inner chamber throbs for the probing of tongue after tongue.

Her ecstasy comes upon her repeatedly and McCaulay wonders at her ability to continue, but Evaline's enthusiasm is far from spent. Like Messalina, she presents herself for the use of every man, enjoying the knowledge of eyes and hands upon her. She receives their attentions with indefatigable delight.

Mademoiselle has stood unnoticed to one side: unnoticed by all but one. McCaulay cannot help but be drawn into the scene before him, but his eyes continue to seek the one who occupies his thoughts. Seeing his glances, she approaches, coming to sit at his side, so that she might speak quietly in his ear, their conversation unheeded.

'My lord, do you understand the desire for pleasurable oblivion, not knowing who is clasped to you, or whose lips embrace your flesh; the desire to be swallowed deep in an ocean of dark whispers?'

She continues, 'Among my greatest loves is the act of being pinned and invaded – not by two or three, but more, one after the other, losing myself among many, so that my identity exists only as "woman": a goddess of flesh and yearning, given over to base fulfilment.'

The thought of her placed now as Evaline both arouses him and causes him anxiety. Her admission, made so plainly, is both a revelation and no surprise at all.

'On many nights I have availed myself of these very gentlemen, in the adjoining room. Each time, I wondered if you might arrive and see me, as I took my pleasure. There is no part of me that has not been kissed and enjoyed. I encouraged my suitors to bury themselves, to obliterate reserve and find the heart of me: to open doors of one room and the next, until no more obstacles remained, and every lock was sprung.'

The vehemence of her declaration astonishes McCaulay. He seeks words for a reply, but can summon none.

Her eyes have grown dark with hunger. 'There is a wild intoxication in being watched, knowing that every man is waiting for me, their impulse holding them captive.'

Her voice, so close to her ear, is almost a hiss.

'At those moments, I control them, through their eagerness to take possession of my flesh. I satisfy their desires and my own, relishing that which others would consider barbarous.'

McCaulay is uncertain of what to say. His adoration of her is unshaken by her proclamations. The depth of her passion is unexpected, but her sexual preferences don't startle him. Nor does her openness.

Evaline, a little breathless, is now seated upon her knees, taking some sips of champagne. She calls forth another who, until now, has merely observed. She removes his phallus from his trousers, fondling its erect length between her ample breasts, so that juices soon quiver at its tip.

McCaulay turns to Mademoiselle, who sits composed beside him, her hands calmly in her lap, as if listening to a chamber orchestra rather than the grunts and moans of sexual labour.

His desire to convey his feelings overcomes all else.

'Do you never yearn as other women do for the haven of marriage? The security of a husband in your bed? Status as a wedded woman?'

Her voice is almost weary in its reply. 'There is enough conformity in the world, Lord McCaulay. I doubt that mine, or my lack of it, will send the planet from its axis. Meanwhile, my heart doesn't soar for the riches you set before me. Perhaps, one day, I may feel differently. For now, I wish to taste that which most women do not.'

Evaline's suitor spurts bountifully over her magnificent bosom, to cheers of approval, and she beckons another to his place. Her breasts, lubricated well, once more set a man on his path.

Mademoiselle turns fully to face Lord McCaulay, enquiring of him, 'What is it that you desire, my Lord? A meek wife in your parlour, to pour your coffee and soothe your brow? What are you made of? Do your roots hold you fast; or is your spirit free? Perhaps you are no more than a feather, tossed on the breath of others, with no direction of your own?'

'I know that I want you,' he answers, the words tumbling faster than he has intended. 'I think of you every waking moment. You haunt me. There's no escape. You're all and everything.'

His reply is excessively, ridiculously, romantic. It is enough to make her smile.

'For that, I'm not displeased. It would pain me were you to leave this place and never return. You have come to love me, I know. It is the most dangerous game, posing the greatest risk; one I've been ever loathe to entertain.'

Evaline, on her knees, is entered by fingers and by cocks, without knowledge of how many gentlemen are behind her, their attentions freeing the flow of her juices.

Mademoiselle chooses her words carefully. 'If I am capable of loving you, Lord McCaulay, of devoting myself to you, it will never be under the terms to which other women submit, for I am sworn to defy bonds which enslave.'

A gentleman's tongue is applied to the rosette of Evaline's anus, circling before inching within. She takes the engorged member of another into her mouth.

Mademoiselle raises her voice in approval, '*Brava, amici! Magnifico!*'

She turns to McCaulay. 'Observe, my Lord; I'm not the only woman to feel this way. How dull would it be to consume my meat with one variety of sauce alone? My body and spirit would whither, being fed on such limited fare. To sample the delights of a great many women is considered right and healthy for a man. How is it then that the opposite is held true for those of our sex? Where we display undue interest in sexual matters, even within marriage, we are thought immoral. For myself, I conceive of such limitation with horror: a torture for which I have no taste.'

Beads of perspiration drip between Evaline's breasts. Transported to another place, she has no consciousness of vanity. She knows only the sensations within her skin.

'*Mia cara, eccellente! Estremamente provocatorio!*' declares Mademoiselle, standing to applaud Evaline.

Seeking to appease Mademoiselle, McCaulay replies in desperation, 'I swear never to hold you to the covenants binding other women. We can create our own contract. I will be your devoted servant, entrusted with your safety and happiness, sharing your life and your bed, while respectful of your chosen path.'

A phallus, thick and unrelenting, smacks at its target, hefty balls swinging at Evaline's rear. Meanwhile, her mouth laps at the salty secretions offered for her delectation. Her watchers stroke their erections, waiting their turn for release in the confines of her soft body. The smell of sexual heat hangs thick.

Mademoiselle smiles, wryly, at McCaulay's ardent promises.

'Grand words, my love. If they're uttered in truth, I commend you.'

One after another, men claim their fill of Evaline. She has no notion of who impales her, submitting to the anonymity of their lustful cocks, slippery tips gaining easy entry, stroking her to a state between wakefulness and dreaming.

Mademoiselle watches Evaline as if in her own trance, one of remembrance and fantasy, in which she clasps her mouth to the bulbous head of a stranger's phallus, and opens her legs, to be slain by the steel of an unknown assailant.

McCaulay sees her lips part, teeth biting gently upon them and her tongue wetting their dryness. He would scoop her in his arms and carry her to some place of quiet, where he might kiss her heavy eyes and stopper the bottle of her desire, which threatens so dangerously to overflow.

He expects at any moment for her to join Evaline in her choreography of abandon. Whatever her feelings, she controls them for the moment, rising to leave the room.

DISMAL CONSTRICTION

*J*n the dark hours, in the fog, Maud can go where she pleases. She can find her freedom, in the cool night air. It isn't safe, and it certainly isn't fitting, but who is there to betray her?

It is winter, and the year is curling in upon itself, silent and introspective. Clouds bulging with the promise of a drenching render everything still.

London is a city of windows, inviting Maud to ponder what lies within each dwelling: husbands, wives, children, servants; the young and the old; those who have much, and those who do not; those with hope, and those without.

Maud's footsteps lead her where faces are hollow, grey, and the windows unclean. The sun doesn't reach this far, into their tedious lives, lived in joyless constriction. In this foul-smelling maze of filth and fleas, the alleys are turd-strewn and piddle-soaked.

Girls barely budding open their legs to make a living, alongside the toothless and rancid of breath. Hair thick with lice, they all find customers if the price is right, against the wall or on sheets well-soiled. Their holes cost but a shilling. Skins grow thick and claws sharp.

Maud quickens her step but she has no destination. She is seeking but, for what, she is unsure. Time passes and she has no answer. Between tattered linens flapping in the sooty air, she spies a slice of domestic lamplight, and claims a greasy sniff of hissing hot-fat sausages.

Her coat is warm but the chill oozes up through the soles of her shoes. She is drawn to the river, and all its hideous, dead-eyed treasures: rot-bloated cats, and cold-meat corpses of unwanted infants, eels plucking at their tender fingers and toes. So many babies farmed out to gin-soaked crones, who care not if they, nor their charges, sleep and never wake. Rub some alcohol on those young gums. Maggot-damp, life is festering.

Maud has been walking long, almost lost to her place in this vast city. The water is calling her, as it calls to the scratching rats. Dense wreaths of mist collude to hide her. The world is hushed.

And then, she sees him.

The heavy vapours shift and dip, as he passes by, head hunched and coat-collar upturned, walking briskly. She knows him first by the smell of his cologne and by the curve of his nose and forehead. If he looks up, he'll see her too.

His hurried steps suggest he is heading home, having tramped his fill. She follows him, her step in time with his, although it's not easy to match his pace. Fortunately, the grey blanket eats up the noise of her heel. He's uncertain of his path, since one wall looks like another and the curb is quite invisible. Home must be nearby. For a moment, the dirty tendrils part, and he sees his way, taking him more swiftly and obliging Maud to hurry, to remain in his wake.

The night is nearly done. The haggard shaft of first daylight parts the gloom, and they've reached Eaton Square. She keeps him in her sight until the last moment. He mounts the steps, and the door closes behind him.

THE LETTER

*L*ord McCaulay sits long by his fire with a large glass of cognac, his thoughts running on the woman who so perplexes him. She must surely endure her own conflict, her head battling her heart.

The next moment, he berates himself for attempting to understand her motives. She is beyond his fathom but isn't it this that makes her alluring? At last, he retires to his bed, sleeping with more reward than has been the case of late.

The following morning, he joins Cecile at the breakfast table for a tolerable repast of kedgeree and poached eggs. His dear sister, dressed fetchingly in dark coral silk, relates her plans for the day. She is to visit her dressmaker in the Burlington Arcade, and meet an old school friend for luncheon at the Savoy; it is to be a most delightful day.

George brings in the morning post and Cecile departs, to ready herself for the carriage. There are several items of correspondence: an invitation to the opening of a new gallery (he will decline); two requests for his presence at dinner (also to be declined); a brief report from his bank, informing him of his current affairs and investments (all most healthy); and a long and exceptionally dull missive from the Oxfordshire aunt, berating the state of her gardens following the wet weather and insisting that she cannot do without Cecile.

She hopes that her great-niece might take the train at her earliest convenience. Of McCaulay himself she makes little mention, other than to add that he might accompany his sister if he has no other business to detain him.

The last is addressed in a hand he doesn't recognize, upon dove grey paper. On opening, he knows who has written, although it is signed briefly, 'M'. That she has discovered his place of residence surprises him not a jot.

> 'We must see how you endure.
> If you have the head and stomach for this particular kind of
>   egalitarianism, between man and woman, we may find
>   a path.
> If not, we shall meet no more.
> Tomorrow, at ten in the evening,
> in the Mirrored Room.'

A MIRROR TO THE SOUL

The hours creep slowly until the assignation. The room is unknown to him, necessitating a footman from the dining hall to guide him. Each of its eight walls is covered in reflective tiles, as is the domed ceiling and, even, the floor. Its intent is obvious: to reflect back all manner of activities, and from every conceivable angle.

McCaulay seats himself upon a divan upholstered in dark leather: the only piece of furniture. Long minutes pass before a segment of the wall hinges inwards and Mademoiselle enters. In her hair, upbraided, she wears a long black ostrich plume. She is masked. Silken pastilles cover her nipples, and a satin sash loops through her legs and about her waist, framing her pubis most attractively, as if she were a magnificent gift, for him to unwrap.

Her shoes, too, are decorated with feathers; the heels click imperiously as she walks. She stands before him with legs apart. The reflection from below is most engaging.

'Lord McCaulay,' she purrs, barely above a whisper. 'Why is it that I'm ready, and you remain fully clothed?'

Her request is soon fulfilled, allowing her eyes to appraise him, and her handiwork from some nights past: his groin is now sparsely covered in new growth.

She removes the feather from her hair, touching the tip against his chest, dropping it to brush his legs. She slowly encircles him, letting the feather stroke his back and buttocks. The mirrors afford multiple views of her body as she navigates him: the curve of her breasts, and the glorious roundness of her bottom.

Facing him, she drops the feather to his phallus, its light touch teasing.

'One day, as Shakespeare reminds us, we shall lie with worms as our chambermaids. Until then, should our bodies not enjoy all pleasures? This room heightens the experience of watching, does it not, Lord McCaulay? Every act is magnified back to us.'

In demonstration, she bends forward, her cheeks parting. She whips the feather through her legs, so that it momentarily conceals her delta.

She remains in this attitude, inviting him to touch her. He considers a moment, before raising his hand to deliver a sharp spank. The slap makes her flinch, then sigh: the timbre now familiar to him. He gives another, watching in the mirror as he makes contact. The sting resonates on his palm. He pauses and she remains folded, craving more. Each burning smack causes the peach of her cheeks to ripple.

He feels his majesty rising, the ruby head twitching for her. He gives a final blow to her flesh, before striking with his phallus, assaulting her, embedding his lust. His balls are heavy with ache.

Wishing to show that he can satisfy any urge she cares to inspire, he rides her mercilessly. Her groan of pain and satisfaction spikes his desire.

Watching in the mirrors, he withdraws his cock, pleased at the sight of it, so engorged and powerful. He plunges again, driving his length back into her. She gasps, but pushes back upon him, enjoying the exquisite torment. The sight of their coupling drives him to the brink. He lifts her buttocks high upon his groin, thrusting into her willing flesh, taking her arousal along with his. He ruts his eruption into her, and she accepts her own oblivion, echoing the rhythm of his pulse.

When they have gathered their breath, she stands upright and turns to face him, tilting her head, lips raised and parted, as if to allow him to kiss her. She places the feather between them at the last moment, laughing gently.

'Truly, your prowess cannot be questioned, Lord McCaulay,' she concedes. 'However, if you wish to enter into our contract, I must be convinced that you can honour your part, allowing me to invite others into our bed.'

At this, she returns to the mirrored door and opens it, beckoning two to join them: the huge African and the young Zeus. Both naked, one ebony dark and the other golden, they exhibit strength and beauty such as no man can deny.

Mademoiselle struts between and around them. Knowing McCaulay is watching, she flicks her ostrich feather over her new lovers' bodies, her eyes and touch roving to their tight buttocks, their biceps, and their toned abdominal muscles. She leads them to the divan, kneeling upon it, one seated on each side, her back to McCaulay.

Mademoiselle wraps her fingers around each fat python, caressing to her left and to her right. McCaulay is obliged to watch, envious yet pleasurably inflamed. She catches his eye in the mirror, ensuring that he observes her.

She takes the tip of the African's phallus in her mouth, moving her lips over its head, and her tongue along its glossy length. Her other hand continues its ministrations, until she alters her attention, turning her face to offer kisses to Zeus' generous spear.

So it is that McCaulay is compelled to watch those lips he would kiss and call his own placed upon the organs of other men. Her dainty tongue licks the shaft of another's cock. She takes the greatest satisfaction in her task, an enjoyment heightened by the knowledge of his watchfulness.

Each stroke of her velvet mouth brings forth a grunt of appreciation from the man before her, which serves to increase her fervour. She intends to enjoy those engorged members to the full, not just against her tongue.

She pushes the African onto his back upon the divan, and strides his lap. Her eyes on those of McCaulay, she mounts the giant with care, allowing herself time to accommodate his great girth.

Lord McCaulay is mesmerized as her ivory thighs part. Her hips make a gentle forward caress then tilt back upon the bulk of her lover. His hands span her waist without effort.

Her golden Zeus, oil upon his hands, reaches from behind to cup her ample breasts, as she rises and falls.

McCaulay's cock has never been harder. He is obliged to encase it, tugging his own pleasure in time with hers.

As her motion upon her steed gains in ease, she lies forward, upon the great man's torso, opening wider her legs, keeping the African's phallus firmly within her, while angling her buttocks.

Zeus has rubbed oil liberally upon his organ, so that it glistens in readiness. He caresses the pink bud of her tightest passage, as she enjoys the column impaling her from beneath.

Her puckered bloom is beautifully presented, eager for attention. As his head pushes forward, she utters small cries of anguish and urgency. However, within the shortest time, her golden lover's shaft has entered. He lies partially atop her, moving slowly, purposefully.

McCaulay's view is unhindered as he watches the clenching buttocks of Zeus, plunging into she who haunts McCaulay in wakefulness and sleep. She has chosen her weapons well, and it is evident that her hunger has never been more acute.

Her impending ecstasy is apparent in the energy of her own rhythm, more demanding and faster paced.

Zeus is the first to shudder, surging into her, uttering a great groan of satisfaction.

The music of his orgasm inspires the African below, who shoots forth with a moan long and low.

McCaulay's sweet love writhes, her body held rigid before a shudder passes through her. A flood of passion erupts, as if she were exhaling her soul. Her cry brings tightness to McCaulay's throat, and his own hot spurting. Despite his release, envy burns within him, knowing that others have taken her to such arousal. Meanwhile, his own seed spills unheeded to the floor.

The three are breathless, bodies perspiring. At last, they part, Zeus and the African taking their place either side of the room. Mademoiselle reclines upon the couch, her chest rising with rapid breaths.

McCaulay knows that he must seize the moment, showing her that his feelings of jealousy can be harnessed to other ends, that her enjoyment of other men doesn't lessen his own desire. In fact, that her performance heightens his wish to please her.

He first pulls the ribbon from her waist, so that it unravels, and slithers from between her thighs. He bends his mouth to her breasts, removing the pastilles with his teeth, unveiling her nipples. Her mask he leaves in place. She lies, fully naked, thighs parted, her labia on show: plump and wet from his rival's semen.

Knowing that he is watched, and caring not, he places his own bare body against hers. Their lips meet in a kiss deep and tender. McCaulay enters a world in which she alone exists.

Her nipples brush his chest, and she draws herself closer, his hair against her soft skin. Her belly pushes against his, and her hands snake about his back, at last finding his buttocks, which she draws towards her, wrapping a leg about him. His rod begins to thicken, pressing at her groin.

The moment is exquisite; they lay quietly, knowing that pleasure is to come and savouring this quiet pause before they surrender to the throb of lust growing between them.

When his manhood enters, it is as natural as a fox seeking shelter in its den. Imprisoning her in his steadfast gaze, and cradling her as the most precious jewel, he rocks against her. He keeps his rhythm steady, refusing to rush forward. Her hands clutch at his buttocks, eager to urge him on, to quicken his thrusts and take her with more force, but he refuses to rise to her provocation.

In this one thing he is able to defy her, forcing submission to his pace, wooing her with sweet whisperings of endearment and admiration, and gentle kisses at her neck and shoulder.

At last, she relinquishes her struggle, allowing him to dominate her. His hands clasp the underside of her bottom, thrusting at his leisure, though with focused deliberation. Her eyes, usually so piercing, so taunting, grow wide and dark. Her body is limp in surrender, permitting him to take her as he wishes. He holds her under his spell now, she capitulating to his will.

McCaulay's lips travel down to embrace her breasts and she drops her head back to expose her throat and torso, yielding to his resolve. His kisses are devoutly tender, but still he grips her haunches, so that little movement is possible on her part. He continues his slow momentum of thrusting, ensuring that each stroke is long and deep.

She has never looked more captivating to him: a goddess he is honoured to worship. Her superiority in intellect and wit is as unquestionable as her beauty and desirability, yet she is his, conceding to him, responding to his commands. Her breathing becomes ragged, and her velvet passage grips tenaciously. She wraps her legs tightly, arching in delight. Sucking hard at her breast, and with fingers pressed into her buttocks, he is resolute in his penetration. They gasp together, sharing the exquisite moment, their souls entwined as devoutly as their bodies.

Afterward, they are like dreamers in half-slumber. Eventually, it is he who rises, dressing silently, and departing the room. She is the one who now watches, until the door closes behind him.

AT THE MERCY OF LOVE

*L*ord McCaulay knows that he is shipwrecked, without desire for deliverance. His love cannot be denied. Her feelings remain, as ever, mysterious to him; he has no notion if she is capable of returning his esteem.

This matters not; his devotion is set in stone, regardless of how she responds. He must fall on her mercy and, despite his hunger to possess her, accept whatever terms she appoints.

Taking his pen, he writes a simple note, which he sends with all speed, accompanied by fifty hothouse orchids.

My Dearest One,
I assure you of my love and genuine regard,
and my appreciation of your independent spirit.
I am your devoted servant, sworn to uphold
your comfort, safety and wellbeing.

If you will allow me to do so, I will become
your protector, your companion, your lover
and your fellow adventurer.
You are my beginning and my end.
Always
Henry

THE FESTIVE SEASON

*L*ord McCaulay hears nothing from Mademoiselle. Each day, he sends fifty orchids but keeps from visiting his club and refrains from correspondence. Once, in a moment of weakness, he lingers nearby, hoping to catch a glimpse of her, either arriving or leaving. He sees nothing.

By day, he walks the streets through which he chased her, wrapped warmly against the wind. Melancholy reflections assail him as he whiles away the hours in Hyde Park.

Winter's icy fingers have entered the city, bringing freezing fog and a damp chill to the air. Those with sense make for Italy or the French Riviera. He feels strongly the urge to leave: to put behind him all torment and find some ease under a warmer sun. He might take a young, carefree girl as his lover, or find release in the arms of a professional courtesan, but he knows such distractions will not suffice. His thoughts will be always with 'her'.

Each evening, Cecile implores him to be merry: to play cards, chess or backgammon. She lures him twice to the theatre and once to the opera: a performance of *La Boheme*, which is hardly likely to bring cheer. He has no taste for dramatic fantasy, his mind being too greatly burdened, and dinner parties he detests. Nevertheless, he agrees to accompany his sister to a pre-Christmas masked ball at the Crystal Palace.

A strange notion grips him that he might see Mademoiselle there, knowing her penchant for concealment. A warm fug permeates the room. As he pushes through the throng of ladies powdered and coiffed, adorned heavily in the latest silks, he sees that they measure their worth by the number of eyes appraising their costume and figure. They are, to him, hollow beasts beneath their trappings. McCaulay unmasks three women with auburn hair, to no avail.

The festive season passes with little pleasure. He purchases the necessary gifts, and makes calls upon those relatives who must be appeased. His smiles he reserves for Cecile, knowing that his unhappiness will otherwise become hers.

After much pleading, he agrees to accompany her to the Barnum and Bailey Circus, for the two o'clock assembly on 26th December. Touted as 'the greatest show on Earth', he wishes very much that the entire company might fall off the globe at the soonest opportunity.

Cecile remains perplexed, knowing that disappointed love must be at the heart of his torture. She evokes the conversation they shared in her boudoir but he asks immediately that they refrain from pursuing the subject.

His custom is now to drink through the late hours, finding oblivion there, and to rise late – usually after Cecile has taken her morning ride in Hyde Park. He lounges at the breakfast table until past midday, scanning the paper (ridiculously reading the small advertisements to see if some coded message might appear for him).

The newspaper holds little to revive him to any interest in the world: the ascension of Queen Wilhelmina to the throne of Holland; the German Emperor's visit to Palestine; the assassination of the Empress of Bavaria; some trifles on the British War in the Soudan; and a snippet on the United States' annexation of Hawaii.

He continues to send orchids, altering his request of the florist only twice: to send fifty red roses on Christmas Day, and fifty white on New Year's Day. Still, he hears nothing, but for the morning he receives a parcel containing a copy of Mrs. Humphry's *Manners for Men*, regarding which the sender directs him towards certain passages, and an illustrated copy of *The Perfumed Garden*, translated by Sir Richard Francis Burton from the original Arabian text.

Lord McCaulay peruses the pages, seeking some hidden message. His eyes alight, in Burton's work, on the thirty-six names for a woman's place of pleasure, each denoting its characteristics: the delicious; the biter; the sucker; the yearning one; the voluptuous; the crested one; the crusher. His eyebrows rise as he reads those words first committed in the twelfth century, concluding that he may have much yet to learn regarding women.

LOST LOVES

*G*reat-aunt Isabella is in her bed, suffering from chest congestion. Her determined great-niece has donned her plainest clothes for the outing, and a heavily veiled hat, tucking every scrap of hair out of sight. She doesn't need or want attention; she wants invisibility. She slips out through the kitchen and Elsie, the cook, kisses her cheek fondly as she goes.

The Great Wheel at Earl's Court is a sight to behold: 308 feet tall and 270 feet in diameter. There are forty cars, each holding forty passengers. Maud has her heart set upon riding it.

Having purchased her ticket, she stands in line, her heartbeat quickening at the thought of being elevated so far upwards.

Stepping inside, she takes her place by the glass, others pressed closely about her, and they begin their ascent. The urban sprawl is in its first stage of illumination, tiny points of light dotted across London, as the gas lamps are lit.

It's too much to take in. Vast and grimy as the city is, from here, it's pure and beautiful. Below are lone spiders, waiting for their fly-dinners, scurrying centipedes, and foolhardy moths, pretty but fragile. Factories of worker ants: all manner of human life, emulating the behaviour of their multi-legged co-habitators.

The wheel moves upwards, the lower cars emptying and refilling with each stop. Suspended near the top, the view is beyond anything she could have imagined. Her elbow is jogged, as someone cranes to see over her shoulder, and small boy pushes past her skirts, to press his nose to the window. Others move from one side of the carriage to the other, eager to see more, to drink in the marvel of what lies beneath them.

Then, from behind, she hears clipped tones. Turning, she sees him, his collar upturned against the chill. His profile is distinctive.

Not long ago, she saw him speak to a wretch she would have expected him to ignore: an ancient, tattered creature, wrapped in a blanket. He stooped and pressed a coin into the extended, mucky hand, and gave, it appeared, some words of comfort.

Accompanied by two comrades-in-arms (old chums, she guesses) he is refuting a fear of heights, unconvincingly. His companions are tipsy, voices loud and pompous. Far from admiring the glittering firmament below them, they are debating a question most sordid and inappropriate. Women tut in disapproval and their menfolk glare, but they continue unchallenged, being too well dressed and too obviously aristocratic to be confronted.

As the carriage arcs its return towards solid ground, the buffoons elbow their way to her side. She turns her back, avoiding eye contact.

They are listing petty conquests now. The man she is familiar with is far more sober, urging them to desist. To Maud, his companions are 'Toad' and 'Newt', residents of the Serpentine; she imagines long tongues flicking out in amphibious slipperiness.

Suddenly, 'Toad' has clapped his hand upon her right buttock, and is giving it a hearty squeeze. 'Newt' is laughing but the gentleman she knows is horrified, leaning towards her, proclaiming every apology. His lecherous friend is far larger than he: positively robust of gut. He attempts to pull 'Toad' away and they scuffle, the crowd parting about them, in distaste.

Only a few moments have passed, but Maud has slipped a pin from her hat and is now taking aim. As 'Toad' lurches towards her again, she jabs and hits her target. Her stab to his groin evokes a mighty screech and a torrent of ripe language. They jolt to terra firma, and she pushes out through the doors.

There is much commotion behind, and the sound of hearty retching: a cutlet dinner and a full bottle of Chianti are splashing onto someone's shoes.

'Serves you bloody right!' her altruistic gentleman declares.

MAUD AND ELSIE sit in the kitchen with a bottle of turnip wine, as sent by her sister in the country. It is quite vile – but Maud enjoys the intimacy. They eat the remaining third of the Christmas pudding and Maud finds the curtain ring in her portion, signifying that she'll marry in the New Year.

Elsie's spoon scoops the old maid's thimble, which pleases her mightily. She's already had three husbands, and that's quite enough for anyone. The first was a soldier who never returned. The second died in a debtor's prison, leaving her with nothing to her name but the clothes in which she stood. The third was a trader in Petticoat Lane.

'He ignited that in me I thought long gone.' She sighs. 'A grand time we had abed; there's value in that when all's said and done. He came to a bad end, murdered in a brawl over a prostitute, and me at 'ome with the baby.'

Maud, accustomed to the universal assumption that husbands and beds are never mentioned in the same sentence, sniggers. Polite Society can keep its delicate conversation over afternoon tea at the Ritz; she'll take turnip wine and Elsie any day.

The cook says, 'As a young lass, I thought nothing as important as the love of a brave and 'andsome man. Just make sure he's moneyed enough to keep you. The young may think they can live on sweet embraces but they won't fill your belly – or not as you may be intending at any rate!'

Her spluttering laughter brings forth a gobbet of phlegm onto the table.

'It was from my own dear mother, God rest 'er soul, that I first learnt the ways of men and how to catch me an 'usband, as is provident for a young woman. She 'ad advice for every occasion,' admits Elsie.

She takes a hearty swig, and refills her glass.

'An 'usband should be plain enough to sit at his settle, and simple-minded enough to accept the stew on his plate, rather than looking round ev'ry corner for a more succulent chop,' she declares.

Maud nods in agreement. 'She sounds very wise.'

'Aye, she was full of wisdom; but mostly gin!' Elsie shrugs. 'All that advice didn't do me no good in the end, since 'ere I stand ev'ry day, makin' breakfasts, lunches, afternoon teas, suppers and dinners. I'll die in me bed dreamin' of blancmanges an' rhubarb puddings.'

MAUD UNPINS HER HAIR, braiding it into her night plait to control the tangles. Men! She cannot help but struggle against the sweetness of the trap, like a wasp in jam. She has been introduced to any number of 'pleasant young men' and all they do is praise her beauty, feeding her a diet of sugar. It is nothing but poison.

She is convinced that it is only in the bitter moments of desire that there is any truth. There alone do men show their true nature, like a scorpion wielding its sting. This is, at least, real: more real than professions of empty and unfounded love.

What is wickedness? Does the body comprehend good or evil in its writhing dance of pleasure? Maud doubts it.

Rain rattles on the roof, bringing sleep. The night hours slide in and a face comes to her in her dreams: first imperious, then angry but, at last, honest and open. If she were to see herself, she would know that the memory has brought a smile to her lips; a smile that would decry love.

A BREAKFAST SURPRISE

*I*t is often early afternoon before Lord McCaulay bathes, shaves and dresses, and thus it is that he enters the drawing room, on the sixth day of the new year, in his flannel robe, to find there seated, beside his dear Cecile, a woman of familiar beauty and elegant bearing. Her golden auburn hair is arranged in the fashion newly arrived from Paris, and she wears a suit of russet taffeta.

He is rendered speechless, failing to greet either his sister or their guest, rather standing near the doorway in a state of shock.

Setting down her cup, Cecile reaches to shield her guest's eyes, laughing as she does so.

'My darling Henry is the best of brothers. I hope that you can forgive his disheveled appearance. He really smartens up quite nicely when he makes an effort.'

She removes her hand, placing it instead upon Maud's arm. 'Lady Franchingham and I were great confidants at the Beaulieu Academy for Ladies. We lost touch some years ago, when Maud joined her grandmother in Italy, but are now happily reunited.

Maud took me to a meeting of the National Union of Women's Suffrage Societies yesterday. She is determined to improve my mind, although I cannot think that she will have much success. She knows the president, the tireless Millicent Garrett, would you believe, and is keen for me to take up the suffragist cause.'

Maud raises her eyes to his. He presents an ignominious sight in his dressing gown, showing bare legs in slipper-shod feet; his hair is shaggy, his stubble unkempt and his eyes bloodshot.

'What a pleasure to meet at last, Lord McCaulay. I've heard so much about you.' She smiles. 'You should call me Maud and, perhaps, I might call you Henry; I feel that I know you well enough. Sweet Cecile hardly stops from offering up her praise of you.'

He is lost for words, not knowing whether to run from the room in shame or leap forward to grasp her in his arms.

Cecile rises, telling her guest, 'I've promised to run to Penhaligon's for a bottle of Hammam Bouquet. It's for our aunt, can you believe; exotic, I know, all that musk and jasmine! We members of the fairer sex are trying all sorts these days! I've heard Queen Victoria secretly wears it, but people say all manner of things, don't they. Anyway, it's but a short skip to Jermyn Street and I'll be in time to catch the late afternoon train to Oxfordshire.'

Cecile laughs over her shoulder as she departs.

'I know Maud is safe with you; she might even convert you to the notion of women's suffrage, Henry!'

Maud is the first to move, rising elegantly from her chair. Carefully, she takes teacups and plates from the table, placing them upon the side cabinet, next to a covered platter of bacon and eggs awaiting McCaulay's arrival. He watches her, hardly able to believe his eyes, or to accept all that Cecile has told him.

It seems impossible that he should no longer refer to her as Mademoiselle. Despite her modest attire, everything about her remains familiar: her figure, the glint of gold in her hair and her aloof smile. Plush and pink, he thinks of her lips about the shaft of his cock.

'I have the distinct impression we've met before, Lady Franching-ham, under entirely different circumstances.'

She perches on the edge of the table, her eyes intently on his. McCaulay moves close, wishing to kiss her, but she leans back. Twining his fingers in the softness of her auburn locks, he presses his lips to her jawline, before taking the lobe of her ear. His breath makes her shiver.

He murmurs, 'I seem to know already, the scent of your hair.'

He fumbles with her jacket; she helps him, until she has shrugged it off. She opens the buttons of her high-necked blouse, her fingers working fast, dropping it also to the floor, leaving her under-muslin and corset. His mouth is on her collarbone, and the upper curve of her breasts.

'...and the fragrance of your skin, here...'

He is more urgent now, his rough chin tearing at her delicate skin. She welcomes him, pulling him to her, encouraging him, her fingers in his hair.

McCaulay reaches behind, to loosen her corset, but loses patience and picks up a knife from the table instead, cutting through half the laces.

It takes but a moment and the abundance of her breasts is in his hands, the loose and flimsy muslin of her chemise barely covering her. Falling upon them, he bites into the generous flesh, burying his torment in the heavy warmth.

Maud's eyes close in the glorious pleasure of his mouth, of his possession of her, of his eagerness to gather her to him.

His hands grasp beneath her skirts and he finds no bloomers, only the top of her stockings and soft thigh above. He could linger there, caressing this tender part, but he lacks patience, bearing down to cup her sex, pushing his fingers within.

'...and the way you shiver when I touch you here...'

Her breath catches in her throat and she surveys him through half-closed eyes. He moves his fingers deeper and she rocks her pubis against him. The warm smell of her makes him slack with lust.

Able to wait no longer, thinking of her hot cunt, he unties the cord of his dressing gown and drops his night trousers, releasing his cock. She takes it immediately, coiling her fingers around the shaft, guiding it to her, as eager as he.

Iron-hard, he drives with piercing pleasure. She opens her legs wider, moving her skirts away and wrapping her legs about him. His thrusts push her roughly against the table, but she rises to meet each one. Her fingers rake his buttocks, gripping him.

Her cries tell him that her crisis is upon her, and he welcomes his own beautiful, shuddering spasm. He clings, his face at her breast, his mouth open in a groan of satisfaction. He assails her with the full weight of his body, pressing down upon her, so that his weapon pins her, immovable. The pupils of her eyes are wide and her breath comes in short rasps.

The table, unsurprisingly, is in some chaos, since she has not removed every item. Her own appearance is in similar disarray: her breasts tossed free and hair tousled.

'Is this how you usually take breakfast, Lord McCaulay?' she exclaims, laughing now and endeavouring to sit upright.

He takes the knife and cuts the remainder of her corset laces, tossing the offending garment across the room, to their mutual amusement, then stops her mirth with a gentle kiss and pushes her back. She doesn't struggle, allowing him to lower his lips to hers. Her hands he places above her head, so that her frame is lengthened, and her exquisite breasts escape her low cut chemise. He holds her wrists there, savouring this moment of physical dominance.

'It was you, I assume, who sent me the books,' says McCaulay, dipping his fingers into a pot of raspberry jam overturned upon the cloth.

Maud only smiles.

'There is an entire chapter in *The Perfumed Garden* devoted to the scents of the body,' he comments, transferring the sticky sweetness first to one nipple and then the other. She chuckles merrily, as he hasn't heard before.

'But nothing on breakfast jellies or marmalades, I'm certain,' she adds, then grows silent as his mouth descends to its task, consuming the jam in long, slow strokes.

He releases her hands to move down her belly, and she opens and raises her legs in invitation, her skirts falling to each side. His mouth sinks to her waiting cunt, his stubble grazing her softness. He laps lazily, as if she were his dedicated plaything, and they had all the time in the world to enjoy such caresses. She surrenders herself to McCaulay's leisure, allowing him to do as he wishes between her legs.

'Mio amore...' she whispers, as he presses his nose to her fur, inhaling her sweet smell, intermingled with the saltiness of his recent offering. Sliding his tongue further, she moans, urging him not to stop.

His hands grasp her plump behind, as she rubs the nub of herself against the point of his tongue. Clutching at his hair, she embeds his face in her slit, crying out loudly.

McCaulay hears George's footstep across the marble hall and leaps up, catching the door just as his butler is about to enter, assuring him that all is well and that Lady Franchingham has simply banged her elbow on the edge of some furniture.

'Very good, M'Lord,' says trusty George. 'Should I bring some more tea?'

'Perhaps later,' concedes McCaulay, spreading his arms across the doorframe.

'Very good, M'Lord,' repeats George in approval, though his face betrays nothing as he closes the door behind him.

Turning, Henry sees that Maud has secreted herself under the table. She peers from below the cloth, concealing her merriment poorly. He helps her up and wraps his dressing gown about them both, laughing into the crown of her head.

'I seem to spend far too much time in concealment,' admits Maud.

'And following me, I think,' says McCaulay. 'I have seen you, have I not, in the halls of the Natural History Museum? And were you perhaps on the Great Wheel, at Earl's Court?'

Maud strokes the hair upon his chest.

'Do not allow yourself an inflated head, Lord McCaulay. Many of our meetings have been pure coincidence.'

His hands find the hollow in the small of her back. 'And now I have caught you,' he ventures, pulling her closer.

'Or,' she retorts, 'I have allowed myself to be caught.' She smiles again. 'Just for the moment.'

'Then I must take every advantage of this moment,' replies McCaulay, relishing the warmth of her body pressing against him.

He decides one last act must be his. He spins her about, bending her over the table, finding her with his cock. He buries himself, spreading her buttocks, that he might observe his motion. It is a sight to relish, his pounding of the crimson cunt of Lady Maud Franchingham.

With a final pump of his cream-coated shaft, he spews forth his torrent, and she utters her own sob of delight.

When they have recovered, she retrieves her garments from the floor. 'I believe your sister won't be long in returning,' says Maud, rapidly arranging hairpins. 'Having taken my pleasure of you, M'Lord, I shall be on my way.'

PROPOSAL

*H*aving assisted Maud into some semblance of appropriate attire, McCaulay falls to his knees, imploring her to make him her slave if she might, but to allow him to always be at her side. Should she wish it, he will be honoured to make her his wife. If she requires time to ponder, he will wait indefinitely (although it is far from his wish).

Her reply is immediate. 'I have no need of a husband, other than as a show of respectability, and fear that I'll never mend my ways, Lord McCaulay; my appetite must be appeased. I hope to have many lovers. In fact, I'm planning a trip to Europe for this very purpose, since each nation is known to have its flavours and eccentricities. I have no desire to stagnate in a life conceived by others, who presume to know what is right and fitting for me.'

She continues to pin her hair into place, peering at the silver teapot to see her reflection.

'Take heed,' says she. 'I am neither an angel nor a whore but when it pleases me to be so. The same, I am convinced, is true of most women. We are as little worthy of praise as of censure, and often deserving of both. Only those who carve epitaphs over moldering bones should attempt to appraise us with a trite phrase.'

She turns, defiant, but, seeing the look upon Henry's face, at once tender and hopeful, and as sincere as she has witnessed in any man, or woman, she softens her tone.

'It isn't wise to hold me too close,' she warns, her hand now upon his. 'I make my journey soon, and go as an independent woman. However, it would bring me pleasure for you to escort me, as a companion, and your sister, too. She is a sweet soul, who lightens my heart.'

'My darling,' he beseeches her. 'In that case, allow me to take you as my bride, providing a veil of propriety. You may act as you wish once we are abroad, and I may ensure your safety. However, I ask that I be present at each encounter, that you may come to no harm. I have spent my years dallying with trifles; let me now prove myself through loving you.'

His proposal seems so bizarre that Maud cannot but laugh. The notion appeals to her as one both practical and novel. Thus, she accepts, with the proviso that she must, on occasion, be allowed her privacy. With that, he places a napkin ring about two of her fingers, in token of his promise.

They kiss once more and, agreeing to acquire a special license at the first opportunity, part one from the other.

'Who knows how many verses we may play out? We may pen no more than a sonnet, but let us begin,' the bride-to-be declares. 'We may yet write something worth the turning of the pages.'

ITALIAN SONATA

The next installment of this story may be read in **Italian Sonata**
(Volume Two in the *Noire* series)

What's next for Maud and Henry? For innocent Cecile, for Lorenzo,
and for his half-sister, Lucrezia?

Towering above its island of wave-lashed rock is Castello di Scogliera.

*Listen to the rise and fall of the sea, vast and inscrutable, and the cold
murmur of the granite. Look up at the narrow windows, and you might think
yourself watched.*

Something, or someone, has been waiting for Lady McCaulay to arrive...

What dark secrets lie within those walls?
Madness, abduction, imprisonment... murder?
The past does not lie quietly.

*A sumptuous Gothic Romance, filled with mystery, intrigue, and the lure of
the sensuous, from the pen of Emmanuelle de Maupassant.*

Italian Sonata is the second volume in the Noire trilogy.

A GLIMPSE OF ITALIAN SONATA

Not far from Sorrento, in Southern Italy, where the coast meets the sea in precipitous cliffs, lies Castello di Scogliera, that ancient seat of disdainful nobility. Built upon an island of eternal, wave-lashed rock, the castle is reached only at certain times of the day and night, according to the ebb and flow of the tides, by a cobbled causeway.

Look up at its narrow windows, and you might imagine yourself watched. Perhaps all old buildings watch. How else might they while away the centuries but in observing their residents. They listen, and remember: secrets and deceptions, memories of joy, and pain.

By night, some of those windows wink, lit by candles or chandeliers. Others stand dark, yet with a knowing glint, reflecting the moon's light from their panes.

Take these stone steps, worn smooth from the tread of generations of di Cavours, and all who serve them. Listen to the rise and fall of the sea, and the cold murmur of the granite. Place your hand upon the castle walls, salt-misted damp, where others have touched.

Like the succulent plants which grow on this rock, the inhabitants of this castle are hardy. Tragedy has taught them to be stalwart. It has shaped them in ways we can only imagine.

Come now, and enter, for a fire is blazing in the ancient hearth, and dinner has been set. The wine is poured, and a tale is ready to unfold.

The past does not lie quietly.

Born with a substantial portion of Toscana in his pocket, the Conte di Cavour greets the world with the appropriate level of condescension, and a readiness to take his amusement, regardless of the cost to others.

Gambling, whoring, drinking and hunting are his birthright; a legacy he cultivates with enthusiasm. In these pursuits, Lorenzo prides himself in setting the bar, since all men of nobility require an example before them.

Even the Italian King, Umberto, in his younger years, was inclined to accept an invitation from Lorenzo di Cavour. Certain members of the Russian Imperial family are regular guests at his table.

He is a di Cavour, beholden to nobody on Earth or in Heaven, or (to his mind) in Hell.

His hedonistic ways continue unabashed as the hands of time race to vanquish the antiquated nineteenth century, and usher in the endless promise of the new. Lorenzo may be of ancient stock, the blood of a hundred noblemen galloping through his veins, but he anticipates keenly the awaiting triumphs and entertainments of this brave new world.

Despite, the vast volume of wine and flesh he consumes, the Conte di Cavour retains, at the age of forty-five years, a rakish charm. His hair, silver-threaded, is thick, and his elongated moustache abundant: oiled and curling. Cigar smoke hangs upon his breath and the odour of a thousand cunts upon his cock, though not yet any sign of the pox.

From Siena to Milano to Venezia, he is notorious for the eccentricity of his tastes, which raise the painted eyebrows of even the most jaded prostitute. He is known also for his generosity, and his reputation for debauchery is matched by his renown for bestowing gifts upon the ladies — and young men — who please him.

No matter that, following a soirée to celebrate the fortieth anniversary of Lorenzo's birth, Signora Battaglia had been obliged to entirely redecorate her Yellow Salon, famed for its sumptuous décor, and furniture made by Francesco Scibec da Carpi (as graced the very chambers of Fontainebleau). The evening had been a relatively civilized affair until a band of female trapeze artists he befriended in Orvieto commenced an innovative performance aided by four dozen champagne corks and the salon's grand chandelier (itself a miniature of those hanging in the Hall of Mirrors within the Palace of Versailles).

The Conte compensated Signora Battaglia so amply that the good lady commissioned a portrait in his honour, which hangs still in the vestibule of that establishment.

Similarly, Signora Segreti has readily forgiven him for the ruin of her collection of rare instruments of torture, extracted from the Stanza di Tormenti, located beneath the Dominican convent in Narni. A blacksmith has restored their cruel workings, though they will never be as they were. The cheerfully compliant contortionist duo of Esmeralda and Eduardo should, in truth, be apportioned some share of the blame.

Lorenzo is seldom fully sober, but when he is, the glint in his cold, dark eyes fixes in earnest upon his prey. It is then that his wolf-gaze is at its most dangerous, appraising with devious intent. He is a fallen angel, as devoid of remorse or conscience as Satan himself.

In this, he is the epitome of honesty, making no attempt to conceal his sins. His scandals, each more outrageous than the next, have appeared with regularity in the provincial newspapers, and, on occasion, in journals of international circulation. His exploits, being always worthy of report, might have occupied every edition, but that the wealthier victims of his debauchery have oft bribed silence from those who would make public their shame.

The greediest of matrons, eager for their debutante daughters to marry into wealth and position, yet baulk at placing their tender offspring in his path. How many fair lilies had been plucked from under the noses of the unwary? To deflower these blossoms is mere sport to Lorenzo.

Having cast his carnal spell, even the most demure allow him liberties, transfixed by the touch of his cool hand, which soon finds its way beneath their skirts. The pursuit and rough deflowering of a trembling virgin, aquiver with anticipation and fear, might occupy him for an hour. There is something in that sweet consumption which warms his blood.

The memory of an upturned face, on occasion, returns to send a jolt to his groin. He recalls the gasps and squeaks, from his having pinched an inner thigh, and having let his fingers stray to places untouched even by the lady in question. A firm hand cannot be denied, and his is a hand of experience, and of pleasure and pain, and all that lies between.

How many pretty necks has his teeth grazed, as his thumb has delved and teased? All cunts are hot and wet in the end, however daintily their owners remonstrate. Their arms have curled about his neck and their legs parted in eager invitation, as they've sighed their protests. They've pulled him close while decrying his damnable audacity.

There is something in that single moment, when his cock, the conqueror of so many, forges its path. No woman who has felt his touch has returned to her Mama quite the same. Skirts and hair can be smoothed, and faces composed, but each young "figlia" totters back to her chaperone born anew; her shame as apparent as the semen dampening her drawers, but with new knowledge and a spirit of defiance.

It is his gift to them.

Such a man takes whatever he desires. Nevertheless, the greatest temptation is to possess what is beyond our reach. Such is the paradox of our lusts, to seek delights denied.

What satisfaction there is in seducing a woman whose outward show of respectability crumbles under his tutelage. How often has he sent a wife home to her husband with the sting of his palm, or his whip, upon her buttocks: flesh livid, smarting with the lash, yet thrilling at the humiliation?

It amuses him to see how far he can push their gentle sensibilities. Will they take his engorged phallus between their chaste lips, those lips which kiss their children goodnight? Will they concede as he spreads their buttocks wide and spits upon their anus, to ease his entry where none has been before? Will they consent to being watched by "his man" (his faithful butler, Serpico) as they rut, panting like a stray bitch in the street, welcoming the advances of any dog able to mount?

How many times has Serpico done more than watch? Fine ladies have basked in the degradation of having his servant's organ in their mouth, and wherever else he's chosen to place it.

On a recent trip to visit his mother, at her London house, what fun he and Serpico enjoyed in the company of Baroness Billington and her sister, aided by three stocky dock laborers Serpico collected on his nocturnal wanderings. Lorenzo was quite tempted to send the ladies on their way, at the sight of those firm and muscular chests, and with biceps handsomely inked. His own knees weaken when presented with so much glorious cock. The remembrance still makes his balls ache.

And then, there is his collection of innovative instruments…but these have, of late, lost their allure. Once his subject is willing to be restrained and pleasurably tortured, they're no longer a challenge. Titillation, for the Conte di Cavour, lies more in the conquest than the feast.

~

Padre Giovanni, of the small town of Pietrocina, has spent a lifetime cultivating his belief in the fiery flames of Hell, and warning his flock, with all due urgency, of the torments that await them for their ungodly acts. He's intimately acquainted with their sinful nature, insisting on every detail via the confessional. Corruption of the flesh he renounces with particular rigour.

As for himself, he feels more concern as to the direction of his final destination than he cares to admit.

How shocked would his parishioners be to discover where his thoughts stray as they bend their heads in prayer? He knows every pretty face and shapely behind, although, he tells himself, these he studies purely with intent to identify which of his female flock might be most cast upon temptation's path.

His own life is one of celibacy, though his hand eases him now and again, when the constant burden of a sinless demeanour becomes too great to bear.

His housekeeper, Maria Boerio, stout of figure and of constitution, has served him ably over the years, fulfilling every duty, from cleaning and cooking to brushing the cake crumbs from his bed. This is, perhaps, his only visible vice: the consumption of heavy fruit pudding in the late hours. It's a duty Maria has performed without remark, having perfected the art of invisibility (a talent honed by all servants worth their salt). Even when the old priest sneezes a quantity of masticated carrot onto her freshly laundered table linen, she says not a word.

Each morning, she checks upon him, to reassure herself that her Beloved Padre, for such he is to her, breathes still. In his slumber, she admires the less weary appearance of his face, and traces the now sagging line of his jaw, the stubble accumulated through the night.

That she has oft contemplated stealing a kiss is her greatest secret. No matter that his eyes are cloudy, and his nasal hair grows more abundant with the passing years, or that she knows the state of his bowels by the condition of the undergarments she scrubs. To her, he is all that a man should be: serious-minded and above earthly temptations.

Like all men of his age, he is prone to piles. Even in this, she does her best to soothe him, preparing a tea of butcher's broom, and an ointment of witch hazel and chamomile. Were he to request her to apply the unguent to the pale recesses of his behind, she would do so without question. Sadly, such a plea has never been voiced.

Her adoration is such that, though she knows it to be a terrible and shameful sin, she has, at times, hidden where she might spy upon him, wishing to behold that dear, though aged, body, in its naked splendour. Enfeebled as it is, the elbows and knees at sharp angles, and the stomach flabby; to Maria, the padre's form is a vision.

Her peeping has afforded her, just once, the sight of Padre Giovanni's penis: a sad, flaccid little thing barely worthy of the name. She imagined her own hand coaxing it to life and guiding it, to offer the ultimate comfort. Such wicked thoughts cannot always be avoided.

How fortunate that the padre is a man of God, and above such dissolute thoughts. His purity is her comfort, as she tells herself, her hand cupping her place of warmth betwixt ample thighs. Her stolen glimpses have sustained her through many a long night.

Leaving Serpico to follow on with the bulk of his luggage, the Conte Lorenzo di Cavour has taken a train from Pisa, through Rome, and onto Naples, before boarding a coach, which has taken him past Vesuvio and Pompeii, arriving in Sorrento by late afternoon. He might have taken a room at the Paradiso Vigoria, to enjoy its lush gardens of citrus and olive groves, looking out over the azure expanse of the bay. In all likelihood, the chambermaids would have obliged him in some amusing manner. He has entertained himself there often enough before.

However, he is eager to reach his destination, the Castello di Scogliera. With the sun dipping into the final quarter of the sky, Lorenzo has boarded a carriage heading to Salerno, via Scogliera and Pietrocina. Already inside sits an elderly priest: an unappealing specimen, to the Conte's eyes. However, he nods in greeting and smiles to himself. He has anticipated sharing the carriage with at least one other passenger, and this white-haired man of the cloth, snuffling into his pocket-handkerchief, has been thrown into his path. Fate will now watch over their journey, if not God (whom Lorenzo has long been convinced looks the other way, if He looks at all).

A few minutes later, the door opens again, hailing the entrance of a third to join them. The woman is dressed head to toe in black, gloved, veiled and hatted with not an inch of skin on show. Nevertheless, the Conte's expert eye, accustomed to appraising a figure at speed and from some distance, easily surmises that the lady is yet in her youth, her waist being narrow, and that she is of some noble birth, carrying herself with a lightness of foot and gentle bearing.

She settles herself on the cushions opposite the two men, spreading her skirts as best she can in the confined spot. There is little space between them, such that their knees will touch, if Lorenzo slouches down even a few inches. She holds her head erect and, though masked by her veil, he would wager 10,000 liras that her look is one of challenge and, even, contempt. Through the fine lace concealing her features, he catches a flash of indignation from her eyes.

It appears that they are the only three traveling. A few moments pass before the driver calls out their departure, placing his whip to the horses. With a jolt, the carriage sways, and they move across the cobbles of the Piazza Tasso, towards the Via Fuorimura, and southwards, past the street-sellers and the first evening promenaders.

Padre Giovanni Gargiullo shifts uncomfortably; his hemorrhoids are paining him more than usual, perhaps due to the heat, and he has a cold coming on. He is returning from his summons to Sorrento by Bishop Cavicchioni, having reported on the declining number of faithful attending his Mass. The Bishop has pointed out that not all of them can be suffering from malady or ill disposition, and the residents of his small town produce children enough between them to compensate for those who shuffle off this mortal coil. Padre Gargiullo is now out of favour, and will not be invited to attend the Bishop's anniversary celebrations. Nor will he be granted a bonus to his stipend.

Feeling thus sorry for himself, he seeks consolation in his Bible, opening it to his favourite passage, in Galatians: *'Now the works of the flesh are manifest, which are: adultery, fornication, uncleanness, lasciviousness...'*

The Conte di Cavour is the first to speak.

'How warm it is this evening, despite the sea breeze. You'll permit me to open the window wider? Perhaps the dusk air will refresh us? It's inordinately stuffy within this carriage.'

Without waiting for a reply, he leans over and does just that, allowing the coolness to enter in.

They pass the very outskirts of the town, gaining a clearer view of the rugged mountain tops ahead.

Padre Giovanni looks up from his Bible, ready to offer his thanks for this consideration, which is most welcome, but the words die in his throat before they can be uttered.

The gentlewoman, sitting so daintily and decorously, modestly veiled and gloved, has loosened the buttons at her neck. Not two or three, but, already, six or seven, such that the jacket of her costume has fallen open almost to her navel. Beneath, where her blouse should be, it is not. Nor is there chemise, nor camisole, nor corset. There she sits, erect and proper, but with the flesh of her upper torso exposed.

The padre's instinct is to cry out, to voice his alarm, to rage at her indecency. His lips move to shape his protest and yet...not a sound emerges.

She twists a little towards him and, in so doing, her jacket strays open, revealing the inner curve of what swells beneath.

Her skin is smooth.

Unblemished.

He cannot look away.

She reaches to the pins at the back of her coiffure, and removes one, so that a single coil of curled ebony-dark hair falls free. With care, she places it forward, to hang against her chest.

With her eyes upon the clergyman, so that he might know her intent, she moves the fabric of her jacket to one side, to expose fully the sweet roundness of her breast. Hers is beauty indeed: such softness, and youth: her areola the palest pink, and large.

Neither man speaks a word.

Keeping her gaze upon Padre Giovanni, she moves her hand, still gloved, to cup her flesh. She holds the orb against her palm, as if displaying, offering, inviting. Her hair brushes the nipple: satin against silk, midnight against moonlight.

She teases her curled strand against the soft nub, and squeezes gently.

The peak grows pert.

The Conte is tempted to utter some word of admiration or encouragement. It would be most appropriate.

Instead, he holds his tongue.

Padre Giovanni is incapable of speaking, his mouth having turned quite dry. His fingers clutch still at his Bible; in fact, several of the pages have crumpled rather badly.

The lady leans forward, her breasts swinging free of her jacket, bending until she grasps the hem of her skirts.

And then, and then, and then...

She lifts, slowly, inch by inch, the taffeta, and muslin of her petticoats: above the ankle of her boot, revealing the white of her stocking, then past her shin and calf. She pauses at her knee, her eyes flicking to the Conte, to check that he is still observing her.

His mouth twitches a little, as if he might at any moment laugh.

She continues, raising her skirts, revealing legs slender and shapely, until the top of her stockings come into view: stockings fastened with ivory ribbon.

The lady, if such she really is, wears no other undergarments besides her petticoats. Her drawers are noticeably absent.

She moves her feet apart, first a little, and then more, until her legs are wide, the fabric of her lower costume bunched at the top of her legs, draping down either side.

Her gloved hands move across her thighs, where the gauze of her stockings meets her naked skin. She lingers there, playing with the ribbons.

The padre's fingers flutter against the pages of his book, and lose their grip. The volume falls to the floor with a thump, its corner catching his smallest toe, extracting a yelp.

As if growing impatient, she pushes her skirts entirely upwards and reveals, at last, the moist fur of her cunt.

The padre's voice emerges in a single shocked squeak. Lorenzo permits himself a slight shift in his seat, tugging his britches into greater comfort.

She removes one of her gloves: unfastens its buttons, and tugs, until her elegant fingers are free. The lady stretches her hand, as if it were a cat's paw, the claws of which require extension.

With all languor, her fingers find the slickness between her legs. She arches back into the pleasure of that touch, so that her jacket falls fully open. Her breasts push upwards, and her nipples stiffen under the gaze of the two men sitting so very close.

Legs parted. Labia parted. Her secret self, parted.

Her wild and wicked centre, her delicious nub, protrudes from dew-sodden petals. With the lightest of touches, she folds back that rose, wishing to reveal its darkest recesses.

Here I am, she declares silently. *Here is all there is to see. Here is what men desire: the essence of womanhood, from which all life springs. Look and admire.*

The padre feels himself both ice and fire: a pillar of salt and of water. With certainty, he can no longer feel his legs.

The lady's performance is now for herself, as much as for them. Her head lolls back, and she rocks against her fingers, first slow, and then harder. The air is heavy with the sour-sweet stench of her.

No more the tease of a slow reveal. No more feigned innocence. Here is her lust, raw and beautiful.

Her breasts rise and fall rapidly with her quickening breath, and the urgency of her task. Her jaw slackens and clenches, her tongue wetting her lips, parted and panting. She works at her task, eager to extract the honey of her pleasure.

And then her gasps begin, faster than her heartbeat.

Her undulations accelerate, as if a wrathful snake coils and stretches in her womb, commanding her hips to writhe in an exquisite battle. A great jolt shakes her, traveling from her sex, through her belly and spine, erupting from her in fierce proclamation. She is a shimmering raven, taking off in flight, flinging off the trappings of her humanity, becoming one with the air and the night.

Time stops for some moments, though not one of the three can measure them.

Lorenzo has to admit, she has surpassed herself, and he has witnessed some performances in his time.

'Brava, Lucrezia dear,' he commends, raising his hands in applause. 'I should have known better than to throw down such an enticing challenge to one so talented.'

The lady allows herself the smallest of smiles in acknowledgement, fumbling with her buttons, her fingers somewhat numb from the feverish flood bathing her body.

'I'm sure I speak not only for myself but for our good Padre in offering you my heartfelt admiration,' continues the Conte. 'How unfortunate it is that we're almost at our destination, for I feel certain that a second act would have proven most welcome. A good hard fuck does one the world of good, and the padre looks rather in need of a tonic. A rough poke of your delightful cunt, my dear, would have revived him no end, I'm sure.'

Padre Giovanni's eyes blaze, his mouth working to express his outrage, but the appropriate words fail him.

Her locks re-pinned, Lucrezia throws down her skirts, and turns to face the clergyman.

'Take no notice of my half-brother's crude taunts, Padre,' she soothes. 'He's a child you know, always eager for novelty. I imagine that you, more than he, as a man of God, appreciate the true revelation of a woman's passion: a flame lit by Divine God himself, and placed within exquisite flesh, to His own design.'

Having arrived in Scogliera, the two leave Padre Giovanni in peace.

To his great shame, his lap is damp.

FURTHER WORKS, BY EMMANUELLE DE MAUPASSANT

Italian Sonata

What dark secrets lie within those walls? Madness, abduction, imprisonment... murder? The past does not lie quietly.
Towering above its island of wave-lashed rock is Castello di Scogliera. Look up at the narrow windows, and you might think yourself watched.
Something, or someone, has been waiting for Lady McCaulay to arrive...
A sumptuous Gothic Romance, filled with mystery, intrigue, and the lure of the sensuous.
Italian Sonata is the second volume in the Noire trilogy.

Highland Pursuits

It's 1928, and defiant debutante Lady Ophelia Finchingfield has been banished to the Highlands of Scotland. A bizarre selection of suitors soon present themselves, but Ophelia remains one step ahead, until she begins to harbour feelings for Hamish, the Castle's estate manager. To Ophelia's annoyance, he's already spoken for, and glamorous French coquette Felicité has no intention of letting ruggedly attractive Hamish slip from the service of her bed. Intrigue abounds, as Ophelia discovers that there's more to her rival than meets the eye, and that the Castle is a hotbed of illicit cavorting.

Highland Christmas

Castle Kintochlochie is hosting a wedding, but malicious forces are at work. Is the castle really haunted?

'Highland Christmas' is the sequel to 'Highland Pursuits', featuring 1920s debutante Lady Ophelia Finchingfield.

A riotous romantic romp, with a mystery to solve.

Cautionary Tales

The boundaries between the everyday and the unearthly are snakeskin-thin. The trees have eyes and the night has talons. Demons, drawn by the perfume of human vice and wickedness, lurk with intents malicious and capricious. Tread carefully, for the dark things best left behind in the forest may seep under your door and sup with you. The lover at your window or in your bed may have the scent of your death already on their breath.
Is the shadow on the wall, really yours, after all?

'Funny, brutal, and irreverent' – Bustle.com
Twelve tales inspired by Eastern European and Russian superstitions and folklore; darkly delicious imaginings for the adult connoisseur of bedtime stories.

Viking Thunder

'We all struggle. We all desire.'
Elswyth is faced with the prowess of Eirik: a giant of a man who lets nothing stand in his way. She cannot deny her sexual attraction and, ultimately, the satisfaction she finds in Eirik's bed.
As Elswyth explores her true identity, she is torn in her loyalty. If she returns with the Northmen to their distant lands, what dark secrets await?

Baby Love

8 months pregnant and still sexy!
Delphine's rat-fink husband has packed his bags and abandoned her for the charms of their neighbour, leaving Delphine struggling to cope. Delphine's

sisters insist that the best remedy for a broken heart is a dose of pampering. Cue a spa break, where handsome Texan Jack and suave Marco await. Will there be more in store for Delphine than a hot stone massage and a spell in the Jacuzzi?
A romantic comedy from Emmanuelle de Maupassant, set in British Cornwall.

Short stories by Emmanuelle de Maupassant appear in the following anthologies

Best Women's Erotica of the Year Volume 3 (Cleis Press)
Big Book of Submission Volume 2 (Cleis Press)
For the Men (Stupid Fish Productions)
Dirty 30 Volume 2 (Stupid Fish Productions)
Amorous Congress (Riverdale Avenue Books)

RECIPES

In the footsteps of Isabella and Maud, you may like to try some of the recipes from this story…

Both serve 8 to 10 persons

TORTE BAROZZI

A flour-free dark chocolate and nut 'cake' – suitable for those who are gluten intolerant

Melt 250g chocolate and 150g butter in a bowl set over hot water. Set aside to cool slightly

Beat four yolks with 150g sugar until fluffy, before stirring in the chocolate mixture, along with 150g of toasted, crushed almonds, a dash of your chosen liqueur (brandy or rum for example) and 60ml of rich coffee.

Beat the four egg whites in a separate bowl, to soft peaks, and fold into the chocolate mixture.

Pour into pan, oiled and dusted with cocoa powder, and with a sheet of parchment paper in the base. Use a sprung pan if you have one.

Bake for 35 to 40 minutes (until a cake tester inserted in the centre is slightly damp) – at 325F / 160C

Remove from the oven and set the pan on a cooling rack, removing the torte once completely cool (run a butter knife along the inside edges to release).

Dust the top of the cake with icing sugar.

STRUFFOLI

Deep-fried balls of dough about the size of marbles: crunchy on the outside and light inside, glazed with honey and other sweet ingredients.

In a food processor, pulse together 700g of flour, zest from one lemon and orange, three tablespoons of sugar, half a teaspoon of fine salt, and a quarter teaspoon of baking powder.

Add 55g of unsalted butter and pulse until the mixture resembles breadcrumbs.

Add three large eggs, a dash of white wine, and a teaspoon of pure vanilla extract. Pulse until the mixture forms into a ball.

Wrap the dough in cling-film and refrigerate for thirty minutes.

Divide the dough into four, rolling each on a lightly floured surface, until about a quarter of an inch thick Cut then into half inch wide strips, and each strip into half-inch pieces.

Roll each piece of dough into a small ball and dredge lightly in flour, shaking off excess.

In a deep frying pan or saucepan, pour enough oil to be able to submerge the dough balls, which you will fry for only two minutes each, in batches (test the temperature by browning a piece of bread).

Drain on a paper towel.

When your frying is done, use another pan to boil about 250ml of honey, about 100ml sugar, and a good slosh of lemon juice stirring until the sugar has dissolved (about 3 minutes).

Remove the honey syrup from the heat, before adding the fried dough balls. Stir in also some toasted, crushed hazelnuts (place in oven for about 8 minutes, on a baking sheet), and allow the mixture to cool in the pan for a few minutes before transferring your struffoli to your serving plate.

To create a traditional wreath, place a water glass at the centre of your plate, coated in oil or butter. Arrange your struffoli around the glass and drizzle over any remaining honey mixture.

Allow to set for two hours (or make a day in advance) – before removing the glass.

ABOUT THE EDITOR

Adrea is a Melbourne-based freelance writer, editor and former stage director. She holds a BA (Hons) in theatre studies. Through her fiction and non-fiction writing, she engages with themes of the feminine, often focusing her lens on the rich diversity of feminine sexuality. She is also deeply interested in myth and fairy tale re-tellings. After many years interpreting play-texts as a theatre director, Adrea is now applying those skills in deepening the "theatre on the page", enhancing the writer's voice through developmental editing.

Adrea's erotic short stories and poetry appear in various anthologies, including *For the Men* (*2016), Coming Together: In Verse* (2015) and *Licked* (House of Erotica 2015), *The Mammoth Book of Best New Erotica 13,* and *A Storytelling of Ravens* (Little Raven 2014). Her provocative flash fiction and short stories feature on many online sites. In another guise, she has published a feminist creative essay in *Etchings* literary journal (2013), and her short memoir story was published in an Australian anthology the same year. Adrea is working on acollection of themed erotic short stories *Watching You Watching Me* and her first novella, a mythical re-telling.

To discover more, visit her at:
https://koredesires.wordpress.com/about/
https://www.facebook.com/adrea.kore
https://twitter.com/adrea_kore

87272825R00093

Made in the USA
San Bernardino, CA
03 September 2018